"I know it was murder." His tone was finite and his jaw muscle ticked.

"How can you be so sure?" She wanted to hear those words so badly.

"The knot," he supplied.

There was more to the story based on how much he seemed to care. There was something else present behind his eyes, too. Hesitation? Lack of trust? Her investigative experience had taught her when to press and when to back off. This was time for the latter.

"Can I ask a question?"

The cowboy nodded.

"Why do you care about what happened to my niece?" And then she thought about what else her police training had taught her. Actions were selfish. People were motivated by their own needs and rarely put anyone else's first. She'd seen it time and time again through her work as a detective in a major city. The only reason he'd care about Clara was if her death was connected to something important to him.

He glanced at her, and that one look spoke volumes.

And then she realized that he'd said the word *they* and not *her*.

"How many others have there been?"

MURDER AND MISTLETOE

USA TODAY Bestselling Author

BARB HAN

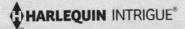

To my editor, Allison Lyons, for being my dream editor for twenty books now (wow!). Thank you!

To Brandon, Jacob and Tori for being my greatest loves, inspiration and encouragement.

To Babe, my hero, for being the great love of my life.

ISBN-13: 978-1-335-63951-6

Murder and Mistletoe

Copyright © 2018 by Barb Han

Recycling programs for this product may not exist in your area.

HARLEQUIN®
www.Harlequin.com

Printed in U.S.A.

USA TODAY bestselling author **Barb Han** lives in north Texas with her very own hero-worthy husband, three beautiful children, a spunky golden retriever/standard poodle mix and too many books in her to-read pile. In her downtime, she plays video games and spends much of her time on or around a basketball court. She loves interacting with readers and is grateful for their support. You can reach her at barbhan.com.

Books by Barb Han

Harlequin Intrigue

Crisis: Cattle Barge

Sudden Setup
Endangered Heiress
Texas Grit
Kidnapped at Christmas
Murder and Mistletoe

Cattlemen Crime Club

Stockyard Snatching
Delivering Justice
One Tough Texan
Texas-Sized Trouble
Texas Witness
Texas Showdown

Mason Ridge

Texas Prey
Texas Takedown
Texas Hunt
Texan's Baby

The Campbells of Creek Bend

Witness Protection
Gut Instinct
Hard Target

Rancher Rescue

Harlequin Intrigue Noir

Atomic Beauty

Visit the Author Profile page at Harlequin.com.

CAST OF CHARACTERS

Leanne West—This Dallas detective blames herself for her niece's death.

Dalton Butler—This Butler twin can't let go of the memory of the girlfriend who supposedly took her own life fourteen years ago as a teen. A similar death stirs up old feelings, and he won't rest until the case is solved.

Mila West—This baby is Leanne's pride and joy.

Alexandria Miller—Her death fourteen years ago changed Dalton's life forever.

Clara Robinson—Could her recent death be linked to Alexandria Miller's?

Bethany Schmidt—Clara's mother isn't telling everything she knows.

Gary Schmidt—He had a hostile relationship with Clara, his stepdaughter.

Hardy Santana—Does this tree-farm worker know more than he's letting on?

Christian Woods—How much does Clara's boyfriend really know about what she was doing?

Sheriff Clarence Sawmill—This sheriff might be in over his head with a high-profile murder to solve and a town in chaos.

Maverick Mike Butler—Even in death this self-made Texas rancher has a few cards left to play.

Chapter One

The normally pitch-black night was lit up with swirling red-and-white bursts. At half past midnight, the normally empty gravel lot teemed with law enforcement and emergency personnel. Dalton Butler's heart fisted as he approached the scene in his sport utility, thinking how much of a contrast the activity was to the normally sleepy town of Cattle Barge. An ominous feeling settled over him. This was the spot where his high school girlfriend's life had ended on a cold winter night fourteen years ago.

As Dalton drove toward the scene, the air thinned and his chest squeezed. A rope hanging from the same tree came into view. Emotions he'd long ago buried stirred, as the unsettled feeling of history repeating itself enveloped him. A shot of anger surfaced and then exploded with rage inside his chest. He white-knuckled the steering wheel as he navigated onto the side of the lot, watching the flurry of activity in disbelief. Why this spot? Why this night?

He parked, lowered his gray Stetson on his forehead and turned up the collar of his denim jacket to brace against the bitter temperatures. A cold front had blown in during the last hour, welcoming the month of December with a blast of frigid temperatures and freezing rain.

Dalton blocked out the image of a young life hanging from that rope as he shouldered his door open against the blazing winds. A gust blew his hat off before he could react. He retrieved it and held it in his hands. The entire scene unfolding before him tipped him off balance as memories crashed down around him like an angry wave tackling a surfer, holding him under and twisting his body around until he didn't know up from down anymore.

A foreboding feeling settled around his shoulders, his arms, tightening its grip until his ribs felt like they might crack. Not even a sharp intake of air eased the pressure. Fourteen years was a long time to hold on to the burden of guilt that he could've saved her if he'd shown up to this spot.

The sheriff stood inside the temporary barricade that had been set up around the perimeter of the tree, a somber expression on his face. Sheriff Sawmill's shoulders were drawn forward as he listened to one of his deputies. Cattle Barge had been overrun with news crews since the end of summer when Dalton's father—the wealthiest man in the county—was murdered on the successful cattle ranch he'd built from scratch. Maverick Mike Butler's rise to riches was legendary. He'd won his first cattle ranch in a gambling match, lost his first wife to alcohol and his bad luck ended there. In death as it was in life, the man always seemed to have another card up his sleeve.

"Sir, you can't be here," Deputy Granger said, extending his arms to block Dalton.

"I need to speak to the sheriff." He had every intention of walking past the man, and there wasn't anything Granger could do to stop him short of arresting him.

Granger seemed to know it, too. He called for Sawmill but kept his arms outstretched.

The sheriff glanced over and did a double take. Stress shrouded him as he made a beeline toward Dalton, stopping behind Granger's arms.

"I appreciate what you're going through and how personal this may seem, but I can't let you walk onto my crime scene and destroy evidence." The middle-aged man looked like he hadn't slept in months. His eyes had the white outline of sunglasses on tanned, wrinkled skin. Hard brackets bordered his mouth and deep grooves lined his forehead. The tight grip he had on his coffee mug outlined the man's stress level. He was on high alert and had been since Maverick Mike's murder, a high-profile case he had yet to solve.

"Tell me what happened." Dalton needed to know everything.

"We haven't established cause of death."

Most of his family might get along with the sheriff now but Dalton would never forget the way he'd been treated after Alexandria Miller's death. He'd barely been seventeen when he'd been picked up in the middle of the night and hauled to the sheriff's office. Sawmill had spent the next twenty-two hours interrogating Dalton, suspecting him of murder and treating him like a criminal.

"Correct me if I'm wrong, but you found her hanging from that tree." Dalton bit back the frustration that was still so ready, so available. He'd go through it all again willingly if Alexandria's murderer would be brought to justice. If her family could have answers. If there could be closure.

Sawmill tilted his head. "Doesn't mean it was the cause of death, and I can't discuss an ongoing investigation with a civilian and you know it."

"Who is she?" Dalton asked anyway.

"I didn't say the victim is a woman." The sheriff was trying to sell the idea that this had no connection to the past. Without proof, Dalton wasn't buying it.

"No. You didn't. She's a girl, not a woman." Déjà vu struck as Dalton glanced at his watch. At around the same time fourteen years ago, Alexandria was being cut down from that exact tree.

"Out of respect for you and your family, for what you're going through, I won't threaten to arrest you, Dalton. But make no mistake that you're interfering with an ongoing investigation and I can't allow that, either," the sheriff warned.

Again, Dalton noticed the sheriff's word choice. He didn't mention murder.

"Another suicide in that tree fourteen years to the day and around the same time?" Dalton folded his arms and planted his boots in the unforgiving earth. "What are the odds?"

"They're high, actually." The sheriff blew out a sharp breath and threw his hands up. "All these reporters drudging up the past, digging into everyone's personal lives. Every story they run increases the odds of a copycat from some crime in the past." There hadn't been many criminal acts in Cattle Barge leading up to this past summer. "There's no respect for the families involved. The people who suffered through losing a loved one and now are being forced to relive the pain as news is being blasted across the internet. They deserve peace, not this."

"There can be no peace without justice. I think we both know that," Dalton shot back. From his peripheral, he saw a woman stalking toward them, so he turned to look. Her face was set with determination, her gaze intent on the sheriff. She had on dark jeans and a blazer. She was tall and beautiful with chestnut wavy hair loosely pulled back in a ponytail that swished back and forth as she walked. An inappropriate stir of attraction struck. Dalton shoved it to the back burner. Charging toward them, she took the kind of breath meant to steel nerves. She clutched something tightly in her left hand as her right fisted and released a couple of times. She was young, early thirties if Dalton had to guess. As she neared, he could see concern lines ridging her forehead.

The sheriff followed Dalton's gaze, which admittedly had been held a few seconds too long toward the object of his attention.

Sheriff Sawmill immediately spun around to address the stalking female, who was only a couple of feet away from them by now. "I'm sorry, ma'am, but this is a restricted area. Only law enforcement personnel are allowed beyond—"

The woman cut him off by holding up the item clenched in her left fist, a badge.

"My name's Detective Leanne West. Tell me exactly what went down here, Sheriff," she demanded, with an intensity that made Dalton believe her interest in this case extended beyond official duty. She wore a white button-down oxford shirt under the blue blazer and low heels, which also told him that she wasn't from around these parts. The butt of a gun peeked out from her shoulder holster. If he had to guess, he'd say it was a SIG Sauer. His first thought would've been FBI if she hadn't already identified herself.

"I'll have my secretary issue a full report to your supervising officer when we've concluded our investigation." Sheriff Sawmill crossed his arms and dug his heels in the hard dirt.

"My SO? Why not tell me? I'm standing here in front of you—he's not." Her determined voice had a musical quality to it that reached inside Dalton. This wasn't the time to get inside his head about why. He wanted information as badly as she did and, at least for now, nothing was more important. If he had a chance to put his demons to rest and give peace to the Miller family, there were no walls too high to climb.

She was getting further with Sawmill than he had been, so, if necessary, he would be her shadow from now on.

With the sheriff's back to Dalton as he was being distracted by the detective, Dalton turned toward the hanging rope and palmed his phone. He angled his cell toward the rope as anger stirred in his gut, remembering the specific knot used in Alexandria's hanging, The trucker's knot. Alexandria would have had no idea what that knot was. She hadn't had a brother or male cousin who she spent time with and she wore more skirts than jeans. Furthermore, every Boy Scout knew that the whole conglomeration could be untied with only four pulls in the right places, meaning she could've freed herself at any time if she'd known. And anyone who knew how to use the knot would know how it worked.

With a quick swipe across the screen, Dalton blew up the focal point, zeroed in on the spot and snapped a pic. The knot could tell him a lot about whether these two crimes were related. All his warning flares were firing, but he couldn't ignore the sheriff's argument. A lot of time had passed. News stories had been drudging up the past. There was a possibility that this incident wasn't related, other than someone being a copycat or inspiring a young person to imitate what she thought was a suicide in the same spot.

"Because I'm not ready to risk details of this case leaving this lot and being broadcast across the state." Sawmill's normally steady-as-steel tone was laced with frustration. "In case you haven't noticed, this town has had its fair share of exploitation for the sake of ratings in the past three months."

"I can assure you that won't happen." The detective's shoulders straightened and her chest puffed out a little at the suggestion she'd bring in the media. The words had the sharp edge of a professional jab.

Sawmill tipped his head to one side. "Forgive my being blunt, but so can I."

LEANNE WOULD'VE HANDCUFFED the good-looking cowboy for taking a picture of the hangman's rope herself if the sheriff was cooperating. Since he wasn't and she figured the two were in the same boat with Sawmill, she'd let it slide and figure out a way to find out what he was so interested in.

The cowboy was hard to miss at six-four and he was using her as a distraction, which had her mind spinning with even more questions. Did the man, who was professional-athlete tall with a muscular build and grace to back it up, know Clara? His hair was a light brown with blond mixed in and his eyes were a serious blue. Under different circumstances, she'd have enjoyed the view. But her niece had been taken down from that tree...

Leanne's heart nearly burst thinking about it. As difficult as it was, she had to keep her emotions in check and focused. Keeping a tight grip on her sentiments was proving more difficult than expected, and she'd put the sheriff on the defensive already because she wasn't restraining those very feelings.

For the sake of finding Clara's killer, she would do almost anything and that included swallowing her pride. The last thing she wanted to do was cut off her best source of information.

She softened her approach. "I apologize for getting off on the wrong foot, Sheriff."

The sheriff nodded. "If you'll excuse me, this case needs my full attention."

Sheriff Clarence Sawmill was much older than Leanne and he had more experience. She was a solid detective, but her emotions were getting in the way and she was blowing it bigtime. The sheriff was already on high alert and, from the looks of him, had been since his town had gone crazy following the news of Maverick Mike Butler's death. Leanne had read about the famous murder that was still an open investigation and she worried that her niece's case would get swept under the rug.

"In the spirit of cooperation, I'd like to offer my assistance," Leanne said, hoping the softer tact would sway him. She didn't care how she managed to get the sheriff's agreement. Only that she got it.

"Again, with all due respect, we have this covered." His tone was final as he walked her toward the temporary barricade that had been set up to cordon off the scene. He seemed to realize the cowboy wasn't following when he stopped and turned. "Dalton."

The cowboy seemed to be taking full advantage of the sheriff's split attention. She needed to figure out his interest in the case.

"I'm coming, Sheriff," he said, jogging to catch up.

Since Leanne never seemed to learn her lesson about fighting a losing battle—and face it, this battle was lost—she spun around to try yet another approach. It was the equivalent of trying to grasp a slippery rope while tumbling down a mountain, but she'd do anything to find out what had really happened. "I can call my SO and have more resources here than you'll know what to do with. Surely, you wouldn't want to—"

"I doubt the city of Dallas will throw personnel at a teen suicide investigation in my small town." The sheriff's brow creased.

"Is that how you're classifying it?" Leanne balked. "What makes you so sure it's not murder?"

"For one. There were no other footprints leading up to the ladder against the tree." The sheriff took in a sharp breath as though to stem his words. No doubt, he hadn't meant to share this much. "I'll include all the details in my report."

"How soon will that be available?" she asked, figuring she was already overstepping her bounds. Might as well go all in at this point.

"You'll be one of the first to know." The sheriff signaled for one of his deputies to escort her and the cowboy, Dalton, the last few steps to the barricade.

A cruiser parked and the passenger side door opened. Leanne started to make a beeline toward the vehicle because she had a sinking feeling her sister would be the one stepping out. She wasn't ready to reveal her relationship with the victim but that was about to be done for her.

"Excuse me." The sheriff grabbed her arm to stop her.

Leanne muttered a curse, wishing she could shield Bethany.

"I'm afraid you're done here," the sheriff warned.

"Not anymore."

"This is my county and my business." The sheriff's voice fired a warning shot.

"That may be true, Sheriff. But that's my sister, and I have every intention of staying by her side through this," Leanne ground out. Technically, Bethany was Leanne's half sister. "So I'm not going anywhere until I know she's all right."

Bethany had been fragile before and Leanne was worried the situation was about to get a whole lot worse.

"The victim was your niece?" It was the sheriff's turn to balk.

Leanne nodded.

"Why didn't you say something before?"

"Would you have allowed me to stay? To have access to your investigation?" she shot back.

The sheriff hung his head in response, and she was certain Dalton made a shocked noise. Everyone knew the answer to that question, and she'd been forced to tip her hand before she was ready.

Dalton turned and then made a move toward the barricade. She couldn't let him disappear without finding out what he'd captured on his phone.

She touched his arm and fireworks scorched her fingers.

Ignoring the heat pulsing between them, she said, "Please, stay."

"What happened to my baby?" Bethany's legs folded and a deputy caught her as she slumped against the cruiser. Leanne bolted toward her sister as her stomach braided.

Even with the best of intentions, Bethany would only hurt Clara's case.

Chapter Two

"Please, sit down," Sheriff Sawmill instructed, pointing to one of two small-scale leather chairs opposite his mahogany desk. He glanced toward Dalton, who was helping Bethany walk. "I thought I made my position clear at the scene, Dalton."

"My presence was requested, Sheriff," he responded. When she'd almost fainted a second time, he'd been there to scoop her head up before it pounded gravel.

"I asked him here, sir," the detective interjected. "I'll be sticking around the area for a few days and my sister is in no condition to offer assistance. I needed someone local to the area to give advice on the best place to eat and stay."

"My office would be more than happy to make recommendations." Sawmill stared at Dalton a few seconds too long before blowing out a breath and focusing on the victim's mother.

To Dalton's thinking, Bethany Schmidt didn't

look anything like her sister. Her shoulder-length hair was stringy and mousy-brown. Her red-rimmed eyes were a darker shade, a contrast to the honey-colored hue of the detective's. Bethany's sallow cheeks and willowy frame made her look fragile. She carried herself with her shoulders slumped forward and the bags under her eyes outlined the fact that she'd been worried long before today. Grief shrouded her, which he understood given the circumstances, and this much grief could change a person's physical appearance. He'd seen that almost instantly with Alexandria's parents.

His heart went out to her, knowing full well how difficult it was to lose someone and yet how much worse it must be when it was her child. Bethany had seemed too distraught to say a whole lot on the ride over, so he'd offered her a sympathetic shoulder.

The detective from Dallas hadn't said much on the ride over, either, and Dalton figured she didn't want to upset her sister by talking about the case. Besides, he could almost see the pins firing in her brain, as she must've been cycling through every possible scenario. He'd watched from his back seat view.

Alexandria's mother had pushed him away and it felt right to be able to offer comfort to someone who was living out what had to be their worst version of hell.

"First of all, I'm deeply sorry for your loss, ma'am," Sheriff Sawmill began. He sat down and clasped his hands, placing them on top of his massive desk, which was covered in files. An executive chair was tucked into the opposite side. The sheriff's office was large, simple. There were two flags on poles standing sentinel, flanking the governor's picture. In the adjacent space, a sofa and table upon which stood a statue of a bull rider atop a bronze bull that had been commissioned by Dalton's father. Maverick Mike had been a generous man and had given Sawmill the gift after he'd gone above and beyond the call of duty in order to stop a gang of poachers. The heroics had cost Sawmill a bullet in the shoulder.

There was a half-empty packet of Zantac next to a stack of files. Dalton had been inside this room too often for his taste in the past few months. Activity down the hall had slowed since the last time he had been here. The temporary room set up for volunteers to take calls about leads in the Mav's case was still in the conference room at the mouth of the hallway, but there were fewer phone calls now and leads had all but dried up.

Bethany sniffled, clutching a bundle of tissues in a white-knuckle grip.

Dalton kept to the back of the room, near the door.

"I apologize again for asking you to give a statement so soon. Anything you can tell us might help close the investigation." Dalton noticed that Sawmill didn't mention the word *murder*. Was he being careful not to set false expectations that he would treat this as anything other than a suicide?

The detective noticed it, too. She sat up a little straighter and her shoulders tensed. Her gaze was locked on Sawmill like she was a student studying for final exams.

"I'll help in any way I can." Bethany's weak voice barely carried through the room in between sobs. Helping her walk into the coroner's office to verify what they'd already known at the scene had been right up there with attending Alexandria's funeral. Too many memories crashed down on Dalton. Memories he'd suppressed for fourteen years. Memories he had every intention of stuffing down deep before they brought him to his knees. His anger wouldn't help find answers. Finding the truth was all that mattered now.

"Can you confirm the deceased's name is Clara Robinson?" His voice remained steady.

"Yes." It seemed to take great effort to get the word out.

"I identified the body at the scene, Sheriff," Leanne interjected and the tension in Sawmill's face heightened. It was just a flash before he recovered, but Dalton knew it meant he'd never cooperate willingly with the Dallas detective. That also made her of no use to Dalton.

"And your full name is?" Sawmill continued.

"Bethany Ann Schmidt," she supplied before looking up.

"Okay. Mrs. Schmidt, can you describe your relationship with your daughter?" the sheriff continued.

"It was all right. I guess. I mean, she's... *was*...a teenager. We talked as much as any mother and her seventeen-year-old can." Bethany shrugged as if anything other than a complicated relationship would require skills no one could possibly have.

Dalton couldn't speak on authority but he picked up on the tension between the detective and her sister.

"How were the two of you getting along lately?" Sawmill leaned forward.

"Okay, I guess," she responded with another shrug.

"Had you been in any disagreements recently?" he asked. Dalton couldn't help but remember a very different line of questioning when he was in the interview room with the sheriff. Another shot of anger burst through his chest, and he had to take a slow deep breath to try to counter the damage. The sheriff had spent too much time focused on the wrong person back then and because of it, Alexandria's killer still walked the streets. He'd wondered if the man had ended up in jail for another crime or died, considering how quiet life had become until recently in Cattle Barge. If he'd been in jail, the timing of another similar murder could be explained by a release.

"No. Not us. Nothing lately. I mean, we argued over her helping out more around the house yesterday. Her little brother is a handful and she barely lifts a finger," Bethany said on an exacerbated sigh.

Again, Leanne stiffened but this time it happened when her sister mentioned the boy.

"How old is her brother?" Sawmill continued.

"Hampton will be four years old in two weeks," Bethany supplied before taking a few gulps of air and then picking back up on the conversation thread. "And we didn't have a knock-down-drag-out or anything. It was more like me reminding her to help pick up toys and her rolling her eyes for the hundredth time. I swear that girl communicated more with her eyes than her mouth."

The sheriff nodded like he understood and then waited for her to go on, hands clasped on his desk.

"We got along okay other than that," Bethany said through sniffles.

Based on Leanne's reaction so far, she didn't agree. Questions rolled around in Dalton's mind. Was Bethany telling the truth about her relationship with her daughter? Why was Leanne so tense? Was she expecting her sister to drop a bomb at any minute? Or was it fear? Was she afraid that her sister would say something wrong?

Leanne had secrets. Dalton intended to find out what they were, because if he could uncover any connection between this and Alexandria's murder he might be able to bring peace to her family. Only this time, he wouldn't involve the sheriff. Sawmill had let Dalton down all those years ago, still was with his father's murder investigation, and he didn't trust the man to do his job.

"How did the two siblings respond to each other?" Sawmill asked.

"About the same as any, I guess." Bethany shrugged again. There was a note of hopelessness in her voice. "Hampton gets into her stuff and she goes crazy. My Clara is—" she shot a glance toward the sheriff "—*was* particular about all her belongings being right where she left them. She didn't like anyone getting into her stuff and that caused a lot of friction in the house."

"Between you and her?" the sheriff asked.

"No. I expected it to some degree. She was used to being the only child for most of her life and then suddenly she was not. She had all my attention before I met Gary." She flashed her eyes at the sheriff. "My husband. She had a hard time with me being in a relationship and then Hampton came along quicker than we expected." Bethany blew her nose and then took in a deep breath. "So, we decided to get married. Clara and me weren't as close after that. I chalked it up to hormones. She was a normal teenager and she was thirteen when Gary and me tied the knot."

Leanne shifted in her seat as though she couldn't get comfortable. Her movements were subtle. If Dalton hadn't been watching, he might've missed them. What was she holding back? Something was making her uncomfortable and she seemed a skilled-enough investigator to know to cover her physical reaction as best she could.

"How did your husband get along with your daughter?" Sawmill picked up a packet of Zantac.

"Clara didn't like him much." Bethany shrank a little more into her seat, a helpless look wrinkling her forehead. "Like I said, I spoiled her with my attention before we met."

Leanne's fingernails might leave marks in that chair if she gripped it any tighter.

"Those two were fire and gasoline from the get-go," Bethany added.

"Which wasn't Clara's fault," Leanne interjected hotly. "Gary yelled at Clara all the time and for no good reason."

LEANNE FUMED. SHE shouldn't have confirmed that Gary and Clara didn't get along. Watching her half sister, whom she loved but would never understand, defend Gary over her own daughter lit the wick that caused an explosion she couldn't contain.

The sheriff's brow arched. He was looking for evidence that this was a suicide and Leanne might've just handed it to him with her outburst. She bit back a curse, wishing she'd inherited more of her mother's ability to stay calm in a crisis. In times like these, she missed her even more than usual.

Leanne could feel the cowboy's eyes on her, and there came a flitter of attraction that was out of line. Leanne had no plans to let him out of her sight until she knew what he'd captured with his phone, magnetism or not.

"The reason Clara didn't get along with Gary is that he treated her more like a servant than a daughter," Leanne said as calmly as she could. Someone had to stand up for the girl.

"That's not true." Indignant shoulders raised on Bethany like shackles on a scared or angry animal.

"A seventeen-year-old girl shouldn't have more responsibilities around the house than her mother." There. Leanne had said it. The truth was out.

Bethany gasped in what sounded like complete horror and guilt knifed Leanne. She didn't want to upset her half sister, but Clara wasn't around any longer to defend herself. Besides, the sheriff was getting the wrong picture. Clara wasn't a mixed-up hormonal teenager who fought with her stepfather and then killed herself.

"Is that the real reason you came to pick her up?" Bethany blurted out.

More of the truth was about to come out, so Leanne may as well come clean. She turned her attention to the sheriff, ignoring the glare her sister was giving her. Another pang of guilt hit. Leanne didn't want to cause her sister any more pain and losing a daughter was up there with the worst anyone could experience. But. And it was a big *but*. She wouldn't allow her niece's murder to be classified as a suicide when it wasn't.

Or to let a killer walk around scot-free.

Nothing would ever be gained from skirting what had really happened, and a small part of Leanne couldn't help but wonder if Bethany was somehow relieved that Clara was out of the way. Not necessarily that her daughter was gone, but that she wouldn't have to fight with Gary anymore over doing the right thing for Clara.

"I came down here to pick my niece up so she could live with me," Leanne explained.

"What do you mean *live*? I thought she was just going to stay with you a couple of weeks until I could smooth things over with Gary during Christmas break. Give the two of them some breathing room." The hurt in Bethany's tone wounded Leanne.

She turned to her sister. "I'm sorry you have to find out like this. But I know for a fact that Clara wouldn't have done this to herself, and if we aren't honest with the sheriff, none of us will ever know the truth about what happened."

"What good would that do now?" Bethany shot back with the most fire Leanne had ever seen in her sister's eyes. At least there was some spark there when all too often her sister looked dead since marrying Gary. "It won't bring her back." Her voice rose to a near-hysterical pitch. "Who cares why she's gone. She's gone."

Bethany slumped forward in her seat and Leanne reached over to comfort her. Her sister drew away from her as though she was a rattlesnake ready to strike.

The sheriff's gaze narrowed in on her. He didn't seem to like the fact that Leanne had been withholding information. She'd been on the other side of that desk and could appreciate his position. She couldn't, however, allow this farce to go on. Clara had been murdered.

"What really happened, Detective West?" The sheriff's dark tone said he wasn't impressed.

"She and Gary, her stepfather, had had a huge argument and Clara couldn't take living with them anymore." It dawned on Leanne that Bethany might not want that information getting out because it wouldn't cast Gary in the best light. Leanne further knew that he'd just topped the suspect list. So be it. If that man was involved in any way, she'd...

Bethany bristled and Leanne shot her half sister an apologetic look.

"She said you needed help with Mila," Bethany countered, talking about Leanne's six-month-old daughter.

Leanne hated the deception, but her back had been against the wall and Clara had sounded desperate. Leanne had planned to sit Clara down and explain all the reasons the two of them needed to tell Bethany the truth.

"I know she did." Leanne turned to her half sister and her shoulders softened. "I'm sorry we lied to you, but Clara insisted you'd never let her come otherwise and she was desperate to get out of the house."

"So that made it okay to deceive me?" More hurt spilled out of Bethany.

"I'm sorry for that. But I also know that my niece wouldn't end her own life. She has a boyfriend she cares about and only one year left at home. Something happened, and if we don't impress the sheriff with that knowledge, her killer will go free," Leanne implored.

"What's her boyfriend's name?" Sawmill asked.

"Christian Woods." Leanne turned to her sister.

Deep grooves lined Bethany's forehead and dark circles cradled her eyes. Leanne could see that she was getting through, and she prayed the woman would do the right thing by her daughter in death even if she hadn't in life.

Then it seemed to dawn on her that Gary

could be investigated when her pupils dilated and her lips thinned.

"How do you know she didn't feel guilty for lying to her mother? Or maybe she and her boyfriend had a fight? Kids do all kinds of crazy things in the name of love," Bethany countered. She perched on the edge of her chair as she focused on Sawmill. "My daughter was mentally unstable. She said that kids were bullying her at the new school. She didn't fit in. I can't remember how many times she threatened to harm herself. I didn't take any of it seriously at the time, figuring she was just blowing off steam. Now, I'm not so sure."

"Can you provide a list of names?" Sawmill took notes. Leanne saw that as the first positive sign. "How long ago did you move to Cattle Barge?"

"We've been here around seven months. Gary thought it would be best to move the family before the end of the last school year, so Clara could make friends before summer." The fear in Bethany's voice gave Leanne pause.

Was she afraid of Gary being investigated? Afraid of the possibility of bringing up another child alone? Or, looking closer, just plain afraid of Gary?

Leanne scanned her half sister's arms for bruises. She had on sweatpants and a sweater with the sleeves rolled up. Bethany had had problems with substance abuse when she was younger. Leanne learned after locating her half sister that Bethany had been in and out of rehab twice during high school. Then she'd had Clara instead of her senior year and, by all accounts, turned her life around. Without a high school diploma or job skills to fall back on, it had been a tough life. She'd worked hourly wage jobs. Bethany had struggled to make ends meet until she'd met Gary five years ago. An almost immediate pregnancy was quickly followed by marriage performed at city hall. Gary had driven a wedge between Bethany and Leanne.

According to Clara, the man was an iceberg when it came to emotion. Leanne wondered how well her sister really knew her husband.

"I apologize for the questions," Sawmill said. "Can you tell me more about your husband and daughter's recent fight?"

"Yes, it happened the other day, but Gary was only reacting to Clara's moodiness," Bethany admitted. It galled Leanne that her half sister would defend his actions. She neglected to mention the times Gary had forced Clara to get up off the couch for no good reason, saying that she had to ask permission before she sat down. Or when he'd made her kneel for hours on end because she'd worn what he considered too short of a skirt. Gary's father had been an evangelist. Gary used the same punishments he'd received as a child on Clara.

Clara was a normal teenage girl who wanted a little freedom.

"What about alcohol or drugs?" the sheriff asked and it was Leanne's turn to bristle. She already knew the answer to that question.

"I found an empty bottle of beer in her room last weekend," Bethany answered truthfully.

"What did Mr. Schmidt think about that?" Sawmill asked, and Leanne could tell by his line of questioning that he wasn't taking her murder claim seriously.

"He never knew. I hid it because Clara begged me to," Bethany said.

"What would've happened if he'd known?" Sawmill continued.

Bethany blew out a breath. "Another fight."

"He'd been threatening to send Clara to a super strict all-girls school," Leanne interjected. "And that beer belonged to Renee, not Clara."

Renee was the daughter of one of Gary's friends. Clara didn't care for the girl but couldn't turn her back on her because Gary would shame her.

Bethany turned sideways to look at Leanne.

The woman shot a look that could've melted ice during an Alaskan winter.

"And you believed her?" Bethany asked.

Chapter Three

"Of course, I did. Clara never lied to me," Leanne responded with a little more heat than she'd intended. So much for keeping things cool in front of the sheriff.

Bethany made a harrumph sound and pushed to her feet. "I'd like to speak with the sheriff alone."

Leanne started to protest but the sheriff cut her off.

"There's coffee at the end of the hall and everything said here will go into my report," he said, motioning toward the door.

It was his witness, his investigation. With no other viable choice, Leanne stood and walked out the door. She'd been too harsh with her fragile half sister and this was going to be the price. Everything had balance, a yin and yang, she thought, except for her personal life, which had been turned upside down since having a baby six months ago. She wouldn't change a thing about her life with her baby girl, except maybe more sleep. Definitely more sleep. And if she could turn back time, she would make sure that Mila's father wouldn't have died on her watch.

Dalton followed her out the door and she could feel his strong presence behind her.

"Coffee's this way," his low rumble of a voice said, and the sound penetrated a place deep down, stirring emotions she had no desire to acknowledge as existing anymore. Her traitorous body wanted to gravitate toward the feeling and bask in it. A little reality and a strong cup of coffee was all she needed to quash those unproductive thoughts.

She stepped aside, allowing the man with the strong muscled back to lead her down the unfamiliar hallway. He made a left before what she figured was an interview room. She closed up her coat, shivering against the cold temperature in the building.

A dark thought struck that the sheriff might be hauling her sister to the interview room any minute. Bethany had no idea how much her actions were about to impact her life, and a mix of protectiveness and frustration swirled in Leanne's chest. Bethany might be clueless but she'd had a rough start, had cleaned up her act, and Leanne knew deep down that her sister was trying her best. Was it good enough? Before having Mila, Leanne might've judged her sister more harshly. After having a baby, she realized the job wasn't easy and didn't come with instructions.

"The coffee here doesn't taste like much, but it's strong," Dalton said, pouring two cups and handing one to her.

She took the offering, wondering why he knew so much about the quality of the coffee at the sheriff's office. "I'm afraid I'm at a disadvantage here. You already know my name and more about my personal life than I share with even my closest friends, but I don't have the first clue who you are." The part about having close friends was almost laughable. Happy hours after work and shopping with the girls had never been high on her list of priorities. She'd worked hard to make detective by thirty and there hadn't been room for much else in her life.

"Dalton Butler. And I'm pleased to meet you." He switched hands with the mug and offered a handshake.

She took his hand—his was so much larger and rougher than hers—and realized making physical contact had not been a good choice. Electricity exploded through her, bringing to life places she didn't want awakened. She reasoned that it had been a long time since she'd had sex and her body was reacting to the first hot man she touched, but there was so much more to it, to him, than that.

From the callouses on his skin, she deduced that he must work outside, which in these parts most likely meant on a ranch. His outfit of jeans, boots and a denim jacket had already given the same impression.

"Why does that name sound familiar?" She examined him, his clear blue eyes that seemed to hold so many secrets. She was beginning to hate secrets.

"My father owned a famous ranch in the area," he conceded as the contents of his mug suddenly became very interesting.

"Maverick Mike Butler of the Hereford Ranch?" That explained why the man seemed to know the layout of the sheriff's office so well. At first, she'd feared he might have been previously on the wrong side of the interview table, especially with the way he related to the sheriff. Now, she realized he'd been there because of his father's murder. The fact that the case still wasn't solved would explain his chilly response to Sawmill.

But what did he want with *this* investigation?

"What's on your camera?" she asked, figuring she could ask at another time why the son of a famous rancher—and one of, if not *the,* richest men in Texas—would have so many callouses on his hands. There were other things she didn't want to notice about him, like the half-inch scar above his left brow at the point where it arched. And the crystal clearness of his blue eyes.

He fished his phone out of his pocket and held it out on his palm between them. Leanne stepped closer to get a better look at the screen and that was another mistake because she inhaled his scent, a mix of outdoors and warm spices. A trill of awareness shot through her. She blinked up, trying to reset her body and thought she caught the same reaction from him as his pupils dilated.

Chalking the whole scene up to overwrought emotions, she studied the picture he brought up on his phone.

"Why is this important?" She shot him her best don't-feed-me-a-line look.

"It's the type of knot used." He enlarged the hangman's rope and her heart squeezed, looking at the device that had killed her niece.

"Which is?"

"The trucker's knot," he supplied.

"Why is this significant other than I'm guessing that only a Boy Scout would know how to tie it?" Examining the knot shot pain through her. She had to set aside her personal feelings, block out emotion and focus on finding the jerk who'd done this to Clara. "Justice for Clara" was Leanne's new marching orders.

"Right. A Boy Scout would know this and that has to be taken into consideration in finding the killer, but the person who did this gave them an out." His inflection changed and she could sense his relief at talking about this... But relief from what?

"You said *killer*. How do you know this wasn't a suicide?" She latched on to the first piece of good news in hours. Hours that felt more like days.

"Was your niece ever a Brownie? Girl Scout?" he asked, ignoring her question.

Leanne shook her head and his lack of surprise made something dawn on her.

She blinked up at him, searching his eyes.

"I know it wasn't suicide." His tone was finite and his jaw muscle ticked.

"How can you be so sure?" She wanted to hear those words so badly.

"The knot. One tug in the right place and they could've been free," he supplied.

There was more to the story based on how much he seemed to care. There was something else present behind his eyes, too. Hesitation? Lack of trust? Her investigative experience had taught her when to press and when to back off. This was time for the former.

"Can I ask a question?"

Dalton nodded.

"Why do you care about what happened to my niece?" And then she thought about what else her police training had taught her. Actions were selfish. People were motivated by their own needs and rarely put anyone else's first. She'd seen it time and time again through her work as a detective in a major city. The only reason he'd care about Clara was if her death was connected to something important to him.

He glanced at her and that one look spoke volumes.

And then she realized that he'd said the word *they* and not *her*.

"How many others have there been?"

DALTON STOOD IN front of the beautiful detective trying to decide how much of his hand he should show. It sounded a little far-fetched even to him that the same murderer would strike fourteen years later. But he knew without a doubt this was the work of one person. And the odds increased when he considered the event had happened on the exact same day at the same spot. "As far as I know, one. But there could be others in different locations."

Proving his theory was a whole different story, and he also had to contend with the fact that the detective was about to find out that he'd been the prime suspect in his then-girlfriend's murder.

"How long ago did the first occur?" Her voice was steady, calm. There was so much going on in the detective's mind that he could almost hear the wheels churning behind those intense honey-brown eyes.

He hesitated before answering, wondering if she'd accuse him of being out of touch like the sheriff had. On balance, she needed to know.

"Fourteen years," he said, expecting her to end the conversation and try to get back into the office with her sister.

"Other than the knot, what makes you think these two crimes are connected?" She stared at him, and he got the sense she was evaluating his mental capacity.

"Same day and location, same tree and same method," he stated.

"The knot." She took a sip of coffee as she seemed to be considering what he'd said. "But fourteen years apart."

"There could be others that I'm not aware of." Dalton saw this as the first positive sign that someone other than one of his siblings was listening. Of course, they'd been support-ive. The Butler children had always been close. But shortly after the crime, his twin and best friend, Dade, had signed up for the military. His sisters had been busy with college and high school. His father, the Mav, had slapped his son on the back and told him the calves needed to be logged and the pens needed to be cleaned, like his teenaged heart hadn't just been ripped out of his chest. Guilt ate at him, even today.

Dalton mentally shook off the memory and lack of compassion his father had shown.

"Have you considered the possibility of a copycat?" She had that same look the sheriff had worn so many times when he discredited what Dalton had told him.

"Enjoy your coffee." He turned to walk away and was stopped by a soft touch on his arm.

"Hey, slow down. I wasn't saying that I didn't believe you."

"Yeah, you did." Dalton had no plans to go down that road with anyone again.

The detective held up her free hand in surrender. "I'll admit that I was skeptical, but that's what makes me good at my job. I don't take anything at face value. But I'm also good at reading people, and whether there's a true connection to these cases or not, I can tell you're not lying. You believe the two are related and I want to hear you out."

"Tell me everything I should know about your niece," he said, testing the detective to see how far the information sharing would go. If she trusted him, she'd open up at least a little.

The detective bristled. "She's in high school."

Dalton set his mug down, turned and walked out. He had no plans to share his information with someone unwilling to go deep. Telling him a seventeen-year-old was in high school was like saying coffee beans were brown.

The detective was on his heels.

"Hold on a minute. I just said that I know you believe what you're saying is true and I told you something about her," she argued.

"I know," he said out of the side of his mouth. He'd seen the distrust in her eyes. She thought he was as crazy as the sheriff had all those years ago. And since he had no more plays left in present company, he walked outside to where his truck was parked. He'd had one of the ranch hands drop it off since he rode here in the back of a deputy's SUV. Reporters had started gathering in bigger numbers, no doubt looking for something to report since news—and leads—about the Mav's murder had gone cold. He shooed them away as he made large strides toward his truck, ignored the detective and shut the door, closing him in the cab alone.

Dalton pulled out of the lot, squealing his tires, although not meaning to. His adrenaline was jacked through the roof at the thought that a murderer—*her murderer*—was still in Cattle Barge. One of the reasons he'd believed there'd only been one murder in town since was that he thought the killer had moved on. But now?

This guy was shoving the murder in their faces. And he could be anyone. For all Dalton knew, he could be walking right past the bastard every day. Greeting him when the man should be locked behind bars for the safety of other teenage girls.

A question tugged at the corner of his mind. Alexandria's killer had been quiet for fourteen years. Why strike now?

There had to be a trigger. Dalton intended to figure out what the hell it was and finally put to rest the crime that had haunted him for his entire adult life.

The one spark of hope was that with modern-day forensics, the sheriff would be able to find a fingerprint and nail the jerk. Either way, Dalton had plans to see this through. Tonight was the closest he'd been to Alexandria's killer, and he could feel it in his bones that these two crimes were related beyond a copycat. He knew for a fact that the use of the trucker's knot had not been reported in any of the stories. He shouldn't read them, but how could he help it? He owed Alexandria that much.

Hell, he'd been the one to point out to the

sheriff that was what they were dealing with when Sawmill had shown him the picture of the hangman's rope fourteen years ago. Pointing out the type of knot used had also most likely helped put him on top of the suspect list. At seventeen, he had been naive. He'd believed that he was helping the investigation.

Dalton was no longer a kid. And he didn't give up so easily.

HOURS PASSED BEFORE Dalton deemed it safe to revisit the crime scene. The sheriff had said that he wanted it cleaned up as fast as possible before copycats got any more ideas and reporters fed them with notions. His remarks were further evidence that Sawmill was considering this a suicide.

The sun was beginning to rise in the eastern sky, allowing enough light to see clearly since the trees were barren of leaves.

It was the dead of winter, close to Christmas but Dalton wasn't in a festive mood. There were two killers on the loose, his father's and a teenage girl's. Plus, no matter how complicated Dalton's relationship might've been with the Mav, he couldn't imagine the holiday without his father's strong physical presence.

A foreboding overcame Dalton every time he

came near the spot where Alexandria had died and this morning was no exception.

Between law enforcement and emergency personnel, there were too many footprints leading up to the tree. Dalton took out his phone and started snapping pics of everything. The unforgiving earth leading up to the tree. The oak from every angle. The perimeter of the crime scene.

He didn't know when he'd get the chance to return and evidence was still fresh even if it had been trampled all over. He had no idea what could be significant, so he figured he'd capture everything and study the photos later.

The tree was mature, coming in at a height of forty-plus feet. It was majestic and had been around for as long as Dalton could remember. He'd seen it more times than he could count going back and forth to town from the ranch as a kid.

This location was between Dalton's family ranch and Alexandria's house in town. He could almost still see her silky blond hair flirting with the breeze on a warm summer night. Her nervous smile. The way she tugged at his arm when she wanted him to put it around her. When Sawmill couldn't prove that Dalton had anything to do with her death, he'd ruled suicide. Did Alexandria have a difficult relationship with her parents? Yes. There was no question about it. That didn't mean she took her own life.

Tires crunching on gravel caused him to spin around. The detective parked her sedan and exited the vehicle. The sun was to her back, rising, creating a halo effect.

"What are you doing here?" he bit out sharply.

"Looking for you." There was so much hurt in her voice, even though her set jaw said she was trying to put up a brave front. He knew exactly how difficult it was for her to be there, in this location, facing down that tree.

"How'd you know where to find me?"

She tucked her hands into the pockets of her blazer and shivered against a burst of cold air. Dalton hadn't really noticed before but his hands were like icy claws. He put them together and blew to warm them.

She shrugged. "This is the first place I would come if I were in your shoes."

"You don't know anything about me," he stated. He had no intention of discussing Alexandria with her. Since there was nothing else to say, he stalked toward her because she was in the way of getting to his sport utility.

"Hold on," she said as he passed her.

He paused as he heard the hum of a car engine on the farm road. The noise was growing louder, which meant the vehicle was moving toward them. It was probably nothing but he didn't like it. He should've heard her approach as well, but he'd been too lost in thought and the winds had blasted, muffling other sounds.

Dalton watched as it turned toward them into the empty lot where all kinds of summer fruit stands had been set up over the years. There was only one time that growers had moved to a different location, because this one had had bouquets of flowers all around the tree's massive trunk and the ground had seemed sacred.

Or maybe they were afraid. Afraid the place was cursed. Afraid a murderer was still out there, watching, searching for his next victim.

This sedan seemed out of place at this time of morning. There were no signs of law enforcement and that got all of Dalton's radars flashing on full tilt.

Had news of Clara's murder leaked? The sheriff had intended to keep details as quiet as possible, but then it seemed like reporters were everywhere since the Mav's murder and especially since the will would be read on Christmas Eve.

Would the media play to Dalton's advantage? Surely, reporters would be just as suspicious as he was about two suicides playing out in the same spot and on the same day fourteen years apart.

On the other hand, media coverage this early

could work against them. There'd been a reporting frenzy after his father's murder and the
sheer amount of false leads that had been gen-
erated as a result had bogged down the sheriff's office.

Dalton didn't want to risk the same thing happening to this case.

The detective muttered the same curse he did,
seeming to realize how little the sheriff might
appreciate the two of them being photographed
at the scene of his investigation.

Dalton needed to create a distraction. But
what?

One thing came to mind. Plan A might get
him punched in the face, but there was no plan
B and he was running out of time.

He hauled the detective against his chest—
ignoring the feel of her soft skin and the way
her breasts pressed harder into his chest with
her sharp intake of air—and then dipped his
head to kiss her.

Every muscle in her body chorded as he
pulled hers flush with his in an embrace. He
half expected the feisty detective to bite him
but then she seemed to catch on. This maneuver
would keep her face away from whoever was
behind the wheel.

Dalton Butler was well-known, but she
wasn't. As long as he shielded her, it would be

next to impossible to figure out who she was. That would most likely keep her name out of the headlines. It was a risky move, though. There were a dozen ways this could come back to haunt them, but time was the enemy.

Out of Dalton's peripheral, he watched a young man pop out of his small sedan. He stood in between the opened door and his vehicle, causing Dalton to brace for the possibility that the young man had a gun, but stopped short of closing his car door. His body remained wedged in between the car and door with one hand on the wheel and the other on the door casing.

"Excuse me," the young man said.

Dalton's hands tunneled into the detective's hair as her palms pressed firmly against his chest. She repositioned, wrapping her arms around his neck and a sensual current coursed through him when her firm breasts pressed further against him as they deepened the kiss. Heat penetrated layers of clothing and caused his skin to sizzle.

He was going to need a minute when this was over to regain his bearings, because in that moment, this stranger felt a little too right in his arms.

"Sorry to bother you, but I'm lost," the young man said.

Dalton took in a sharp breath before pulling

back. As he looked at the man, he saw a camera being aimed at him.

"Don't turn around," he said under his breath to the detective before looking straight at the guy who had to be a reporter. "What the hell do you want?"

"Nothing," the startled voice said in reaction to Dalton's tone. "I already got what I came for."

Chapter Four

"Dammit," Dalton said, cursing again under his breath. "Keep your face covered in case he tries to shoot another picture."

The reporter hopped into his sedan and then tore out of the parking lot, spewing gravel. Before the small gray car could disappear, Dalton palmed his own phone and snapped a pic of the back of the vehicle. He'd open his own investigation on the man and see what he could find.

"This isn't good," the detective said. "I could lose my job if this thing plays out wrong."

"We need to go." Dalton started toward his sport utility, feeling a cold blast of morning air penetrate his thin jacket.

"Where?" Detective West asked.

"You can go wherever you want," he shot back. Other than engaging in a kiss that did a little too much damage to his senses, nothing had changed. She still didn't trust him, a sentiment that went both ways.

"The sheriff said there was only one set of footprints leading up to the base of the tree before she was taken down. Now there are many," she said and her words stopped Dalton in his tracks.

"How much did your niece weigh?" he asked.

Leanne must've known the question was coming because she answered without hesitation. "Around a hundred pounds or so."

"He could've carried her," he countered, keeping his back to her. He stomped on the ground. The earth was cold, hard, unforgiving. "I'm a big guy and I'm barely leaving a footprint."

"I'm trying to talk the sheriff into treating this as a murder investigation," she said. "Maybe if you come with me, I'll have a chance."

"Being with me will only hurt your cause in case you haven't noticed." Dalton needed to get back to the ranch where he could be productive. Besides, he wanted to examine the pictures he'd taken in detail. "Good luck."

There were no sounds of footprints behind him, which meant the detective was standing her ground. "If Sawmill treats this as a suicide, we both lose."

"He won't change his mind and especially not with me around," Dalton said. "It's a matter of pride at this point."

"Then we have to think of a way to change

it for him." The despair in her voice nearly cracked the casing that locked down his emotions. He'd buried them so deep in order to survive all these years he was caught off guard that anyone could come close enough to touching that place inside him.

"You've never met the guy. He'll stay the course," he said.

She shot him a curious glance and he decided not to go into detail about how he knew Sawmill so well. "We need him. I can't call in favors in Dallas to investigate leads. Not without putting people's jobs in jeopardy and I won't do that to my friends. If you and I put our heads together, we might just get somewhere."

"I have to go to work," Dalton said, figuring he'd given enough of his time to this lost cause. If she thought he could make an impact with Sawmill, she'd have a better chance without his involvement. That part was true enough.

"My niece is dead because of me. It's my fault. I should've been here. We were supposed to meet and I was late." Damn, the sound of anguish in her words tugged at him. It was a pull he couldn't afford. He should walk away right now and not look back.

Instead, he turned around, wishing there was something he could say to ease her pain. "Blaming yourself won't bring her back. Believe me."

"Who did that tree take from you?" she asked, and her eyes here wide bright brown orbs.

Dalton started to answer but held back.

"I'll find out either way. I'm sure there's been coverage, and I still have resources at the department who can check into a cold case. Why not just tell me and make this easier on both of us?" she asked.

Trying to force his hand was as productive as trying to drink milk from a snake.

"Because it's none of your damn business." A surprising explosion of anger rattled against his chest. His blood pressure spiked and adrenaline-heated blood coursed through him.

A grunt-like noise issued from the detective. "This whole situation stinks for both of us, but this could go easier if we work together. And you might just get the answers you need as desperately as I do."

"Good luck, Detective." He walked away.

She stalked behind him and poked him on the shoulder.

Dalton stopped but didn't turn.

"Name your price. I'll do whatever it takes to get your help."

Damn that he was about to agree to help her.

LEANNE WALKED INTO Sawmill's office ahead of the tall cowboy. She didn't like the way she could feel his masculine presence behind her without needing to see him. She chalked it up to his intensity and did her level best to move on.

"Thank you for agreeing to see us again, Sheriff." Leanne held her hand out.

Sawmill politely shook it and greeted them but stopped short of inviting them to sit this time. He stood near the door, making it all too clear that he had nothing else to add and expected this meeting to last a minute or two at best. From the grooves around his eyes, she sensed that his patience was running thin.

"I appreciate how much you have on your plate right now..." she started but was met with a get-on-with-it response in the form of the sheriff leaning back on his heels.

Okay, she could work with his emotions. See if she could get his agreement to move forward with a murder investigation instead of wrapping this case as a suicide.

"We just came from the scene," Leanne said, figuring the sheriff needed to be aware since the guy who was most likely a reporter had taken a picture of them. "Someone showed up and had his phone out. I'm sure he took a picture but we did what we could to hide my face. The story could leak."

The news didn't seem to sit well with the sheriff. He folded his arms in a defensive tactic. He was shoring up his reserves when she was trying to lower his guard by sharing and being honest. All she needed was his word that he would open an investigation.

"I'm sorry about that. It's not good if my name is linked to the scene and I know it," she quickly added.

"What were you doing at my scene? What's the real reason you requested this meeting?" Sawmill asked.

When Leanne hesitated, he added, "I don't have the resources to follow every bunny trail, including professional courtesy cases. If I did, I'd be more than happy…"

"This isn't a case of departmental cooperation or respect. I have no intention of wasting your resources or time." Leanne shouldn't allow herself to become so heated, but this was Clara. Her sweet niece was never coming back and she knew in her heart Clara hadn't committed suicide. Leanne suppressed a sob. "I know for a fact that my niece never would've done this to herself."

"I'm listening," the sheriff said. His posture had improved; she had his ear and she wouldn't look a gift horse in the mouth by overanalyzing it.

"Gary didn't like her," she added, fighting the personal disdain she had for her brother-in-law.

"That's nothing new in my business," Sawmill responded flatly. Any hope she had that he could be taking her seriously fizzled.

"Of course it isn't, but how often do you have a detective telling you there are holes in your case?" she said a little indignant. Damn, why'd she say that? Putting Sawmill on the defensive would only move him further away from her goal.

Dalton touched her arm and heat crackled at the point of contact. "We're done here. He won't take you seriously."

"Whatever's between us happened in the past, Mr. Butler. This has nothing to do with it." Sawmill was really on the defensive now. Dalton had struck a chord. She hadn't thought bringing him into the equation would actually hurt her case, even though he'd insisted that it would.

"We don't need him to find out what happened," Dalton said, and his commanding voice sent another jolt rocketing through her, a jolt that couldn't be more inappropriate under the circumstances.

"I do. I have no intention of working outside the law or putting my career on the line no matter how personal this case is," she shot back. That was mostly true. She was willing to stretch boundaries when the time was right, but she wasn't anywhere near there yet.

"There's no incentive for him to open another murder investigation he can't solve." Now the cowboy had stepped on the sheriff's toes.

But then her rational appeals were netting zero.

"All the resources I have are invested in keeping this town safe while I track down a killer," Sawmill defended. "A suicide—" he flashed his eyes at Leanne "—no matter how upsetting or personal the case might be, has no place sitting in a murder jacket."

"Are you calling me a liar?" Leanne was taken aback.

"I'm saying that your judgment is compromised and I don't blame you. There's a reason it's against department policy to work on a conflict-of-interest case in every law enforcement agency in the country," he said, again with that even tone.

It infuriated Leanne, but Dalton touched her arm once more and the spark distracted her for a split second.

"Who knows, you just might solve two cases at once. Forensics has come a long way," Dalton continued and she was pretty sure the sheriff's ruddy complexion became even rosier, another sign this meeting was going south. He was right about one thing. Keeping her emotions in check was going to be more difficult than she'd estimated.

"It has." The sheriff's tone was steadfast.

"Then we're wasting our time here like I said before." There was anger in his voice now as he spoke to the sheriff. "If you won't believe a detective, I have no chance of convincing you. Besides, I tried once and we both know how that turned out."

"These cases aren't related," Sawmill said.

"Really?" Dalton took a step back. "Same method. Same tree. Same knot. Hell, it was the same day at around the same time. Are you planning to look me in the eye and tell me this is a coincidence?"

Sawmill stared at him but said nothing at first.

And Leanne figured she and Dalton were about to be escorted out the way they had come in when the sheriff lifted his gaze to meet the handsome rancher's.

He stared for a long moment without saying a word.

And then he issued a sharp sigh. "I owe it to you to take this seriously, Dalton. One of my deputies will pull her cell phone records. We'll see who she was talking to leading up to last night. There are a few other pieces of evidence I can have processed. If anything comes up to change my initial opinion, you have my word I'll open a criminal investigation. Between now and then, I'd like to keep this as quiet as possible."

This was a huge win and she had no plans to push her luck. "Thank you, sir."

"Let's see if there's anything there to be concerned with." He held up his hands, palms out.

"Anything you can do is appreciated," Dalton said before escorting Leanne out of the building.

Neither spoke until they reached the safety of the sport utility.

"It's obvious that you two have history. Do you plan on telling me what any of that was about?"

The doors were locked and the windows were up.

Dalton turned the key in the ignition. "I'd rather talk about our next step. You shouldn't leave your car at the lot today."

"What are the chances we can go back to get it unnoticed?" She wondered how much damage there'd be if her name was linked to the case.

"Slim. Especially now that the sun has come up."

"Did he get my license plate?" Leaving her car there could pose a problem, too.

"Not that I could tell. I was a little preoccupied." She could've sworn a small smirk dented the corner of his lips.

If it did, he suppressed it just as quickly.

She'd been thinking about that kiss, about the contrast of his hard, muscled chest and the tenderness he'd shown when he pressed his lips to hers. About how good he tasted, like coffee and mint…and she shouldn't be thinking these destructive thoughts right now.

"Where should we go?" She bit back a yawn.

"I'll drop you off anywhere you want," he said.

"Can we talk through what happened while the details are fresh?" she asked.

"The ranch needs me," he said.

What was he up to?

"I can drop you off at your sister's," he said.

"After the way we left things, I doubt it," she responded. "And since I'll be sticking around a few days, I'll need a recommendation for a place to stay while my sister cools off."

There was no way Bethany was going to give Leanne access to Clara's room after everything she'd said to her half sister.

Besides, Gary had most likely torn it apart already.

THE BLACK COFFEE burned Dalton's throat as he took a sip. It felt good. Reminded him that he was alive. He took another, still trying to figure out what he was doing with Leanne West when he should've dropped her off so he could examine the photos on his phone in privacy. But then a part of him realized she had a right to know if he found something there. Besides, with her trained eye, she could be useful in evaluating them.

"Thanks for not dropping me off and leaving," the detective said. "And for everything you've been doing to help so far. I never would've gotten that far with the sheriff on my own."

Dalton nodded.

The detective ran her index finger along the rim of her coffee cup. She took hers with cream and two packets of raw sugar. He didn't want to notice those details about her. She wasn't a date. And even the women he'd spent time with never stayed long enough for him to figure out their coffee habits. He knew very little about the woman sitting across the booth from him in the empty café off the highway.

There were other details he'd cataloged about her. The fact that she didn't wear a wedding ring. He told himself the only reason he noticed was because of the kiss—a kiss so hot he didn't need to think about it, either—and a necessary apology that would have gone to her husband if she'd had one.

Dalton set his cup down. He also noticed that she'd picked at the hem of her navy blazer four times since sitting down and figured she was nervous. Was it because she was with him?

"If we're going to work together, we should probably know some basics about each other, Detective," he started, figuring information might come in handy if they somehow separated.

The detective blew out a burst of air. "Okay. First things first, call me Leanne."

He nodded.

"I'm from Dallas, but you already know that. I have a six-month-old daughter." She paused long enough to pull out her cell phone and show him a pic of a partially toothed little girl. "Mila."

"Cute kid," he said. His newly found half brother, Wyatt, had a six-month-old kid.

"There's no father," she said with an awkward half smile. "I mean, there was a father, but he's not…*around.*"

"He's an idiot," Dalton said before he could stop himself. He probably shouldn't insult a man he didn't know, but anyone who could walk out on a face like the one on the cell phone and not look back had to be a first-order jerk.

Leanne shot a warning look, which surprised him and told him there was more to the story. "My neighbor has been a gift. She loves kids, has more grandkids than I have fingers on one hand and she's keeping Mila for a few days."

"Sounds like a good setup."

She nodded. "Other than that, there's not much to tell. I worked my butt off to make detective before thirty. I've been on the job two years, so still earning my stripes to some." And then turned the tables on him. "What's your story?"

"You already know my name is Dalton Butler. I have a twin, Dade. We're identical, so if you bump into someone who looks a helluva lot like me but says he's not, he's not lying." He chuckled at her wide eyes. "What? You've never met twins before?"

She made a gesture. "I guess I have. Haven't known a lot personally."

"My father was fairly famous in Texas." He paused before adding, "Infamous in some circles."

"I heard a lot of good things about him," she said casually, like it was common knowledge.

She obviously didn't know the real man. But then, who really did?

"I'm one of six kids, unless someone else comes out of the woodwork before the reading of the Mav's will on Christmas Eve." He tried to suppress the anger in his voice and figured he wasn't doing a great job based on the look she shot him. "Four of us grew up under one roof and had the same mother."

"Do you work on the farm?" she asked.

"It's a ranch. And the answer is yes," he said indignantly, picking up a packet of sugar. He should've realized a Dallas detective wouldn't know much about ranching but calling Hereford a farm was a lot like calling a horse a cow. "All of us do in some capacity, including the new ones."

A moment of silence passed between the two of them before Leanne's gaze intensified.

"Why do you care so much about this case?" She pinned him with her stare, and he couldn't tell if she was looking at him or through him. "Who did you lose?"

"It's been fourteen years, so the number fourteen might be important," he said, redirecting the conversation. He tossed the sugar packet on top of the table.

Leanne sat there for a long moment, like she was expecting—hoping?—he'd return to the original conversation thread. She'd have to figure it out as they went along. He had no plans to rush. Drudging up that pain held no interest to Dalton.

On a resigned-sounding sigh, she pulled a small notepad and pen out of her purse.

"Fourteen," she parroted as she jotted the number down. "The date might be significant."

She wrote, *December 7.*

"Also, the digital date of twelve-seven," he added.

"Right. The tree is oak." She twirled the pen around her fingers and shot an anxious look at Dalton. "He put them on display."

He could see that she was trying to hold back a flood of emotions.

"He likes to show his work," Dalton ground out through clenched back teeth.

"Because he wants the bodies to be found." Leanne gripped the pen and removed the cap before replacing it. Nervous tick? Or was this one of her little habits when she concentrated?

Dalton broke eye contact and focused on the black liquid in his cup. Anger was an out-of-control tide rising inside him. One he needed to get under control.

"He likes young girls," Leanne said. "Was your friend in high school?"

A sharp sigh issued. If the two of them were going to come up with a profile of the killer, he needed to talk about her. Although, nothing inside him wanted to. *Do it for Alexandria*, a little voice in the back of his mind said.

"A junior," he said and those two words were harder to say than he figured they would be.

"So was Clara. She was already making plans for senior year," she said, and her voice was anguished.

There was a pull toward it, maybe because it mimicked his own pain.

"Your niece. Was she blonde, like her mother?" he asked. "And alone on the night of the seventh?"

"Yes and yes, but everything about Clara was full of life. My sister—" she paused long enough to look up at him "—half sister used to look more like her daughter based on the pictures I've seen of her. Now, she's just faded, washed-out. Exhausted."

"The two of you didn't grow up in the same house?" he asked.

"No. We have different mothers. Our father was some piece of work." She rolled her eyes and embarrassment flushed her cheeks.

"How'd the two of you meet?"

"I tracked her down after my mother passed away when I was a rookie. Before then she'd asked me not to try to find my father. Looking for siblings felt like a betrayal and that last year with Mother's cancer was hard." Leanne looked flustered. "My sister was a mess when I found her, but then we got her into rehab and she cleaned up her act."

"Speaking of your family, the sheriff will follow up with your brother-in-law," he said.

"I'd expect him to," she said in that determined voice he was beginning to recognize.

"What are the odds he'll find something there?" Dalton had to ask.

Leanne stared out the window for a long moment.

"They'd better be slim-to-none," she finally said through gritted teeth. "What kind of clothing was your girlfriend wearing?"

"I never said she was my girlfriend," he countered.

"You didn't have to." There was compassion in her voice now. No trace of the rage he'd heard when she spoke of her brother-in-law. "This is deeply personal for you and that's the only reason you care about my niece's case. Don't get me wrong, I'll take all the help I can get, but based on your reaction so far I'd say the two of you used to be close."

Perceptive.

"We dated in high school. I'm the reason she was in that lot in the first place. She was waiting for me but I was out partying, having a good time. We'd had a dustup over my drinking, so I didn't want to show up with alcohol on my breath." Damn, those words were bitter tasting as they passed over his lips. "I left her there alone. By the time I show up, it was too late. Since I was the last person she'd seen and the first to find her—"

"You were the only suspect," she cut him off.

"That's right," he said.

"And that's the undercurrent I feel between you and the sheriff," she added.

"That and the fact that he still hasn't found my father's murderer." Dalton took another sip of coffee.

Her cup suddenly became very interesting to her. "I'm sorry about your friend. And I'm so sorry that you lost someone you cared about, especially while you were so young. This situation would be difficult for anyone, but a teenager…"

Dalton acknowledged her sentiment but nothing could ease the pain.

Leanne didn't speak. She looked up at him and caught his gaze, searching his eyes for something. A sign that it was okay to move on?

He nodded slightly to prod her into speaking again. At least for the moment, he had no more words ready.

"We'll come back to clothing. So, this person likes seventeen-year-old girls. Both events happened on the same day in December but fourteen years apart. The timing has to be significant."

"There was no sign of struggle at either scene,"

he added in a shaky voice—unsteady from anger. "I've gone off the assumption we're looking for a man all these years. You see anything to give me another direction?"

"No. A male is a safe assumption. I mean, cases like these are almost always male. This person had to be strong enough to hoist her up." Leanne's voice broke and a tear slid down her cheek. She seemed caught off guard. "Sorry."

Dalton reached across the table and thumbed it away. A hum of electricity pulsed through him at the contact and he bit back a curse. He resisted the urge to tuck the few tendrils of loose hair behind her ears.

Solving Alexandria's case was priority number one.

He needed to keep the thought close, because his damn hands wanted to reach for the beautiful determined woman across the table.

It was a case of sympathy, two people in a rare but similar circumstance. Or maybe a primal need for proof of life had him wanting to be her comfort. There was no way real feelings could be developing, considering he'd known the woman less than twenty-four hours.

Or could there?

Chapter Five

Both Leanne and Dalton had ordered, the food had arrived and she was doing more rearranging bites on her plate than actual eating. She'd ordered a full Southern breakfast of eggs and bacon along with biscuits and gravy mostly to appease Dalton, who seemed determined to get a warm calorie-laden meal inside her. The smell of food turned her stomach and she missed her little girl so much she ached. Despite working a full-time job, Leanne had been the one to put Mila to bed every night since her daughter was born six months ago and her heart wanted to be there for her daughter more.

If Leanne hadn't been so preoccupied with her newborn, she might've read the signs of trouble within Clara more accurately. A now-familiar pang of guilt struck deep and hard.

"Mind if we review your pictures?" she asked. The pain was never far from her thoughts and she needed to distract herself by maintaining focus on the case, on finding Clara's killer rather than being caught up in her emotions. The sheriff had made a good point. There was a reason investigators didn't work cases when a conflict of interest was present. The legal implications were only one part of the problem. Emotions were the other bigger issue. Get too caught up in her feelings and she could miss something important, something that could crack the case wide open.

Dalton studied her plate and she got the message. He wanted her to eat. But how could she? Her niece was gone and the person responsible was walking around free.

Pushing a clump of overcooked egg with her fork, she said, "I'm not hungry." Before he could protest, she added, "Mind if I sit on your side?"

Dalton shook his head.

Leanne came around the booth and slid in beside him. Her left arm grazed his right, reminding her how bad of an idea making physical contact with him was. Even through layers of clothes and jackets, there was a spark of attraction along with a free-falling sensation in her stomach.

"I shot everything I could think of, so there's a lot on here and I can't guarantee any of these will be useful," he warned.

"Let's just go through them one by one."

She picked up her coffee cup and held it in two hands, appreciating the warmth on her palms.

"I hoped there might be something here to tie the crimes together," Dalton said. "But fourteen years is a long time and I don't have any photos from the original scene."

"The sheriff does. Maybe we can convince him to let us take a look at those. Compare."

"Doubt it. Do they even keep evidence from a suicide?" he asked.

"Good point. Every agency is different. We need to figure out a way to get him to check the database to see if there have been any other similar crimes in the past fourteen years." She was trying to offer hope. Losing her niece as an adult was horrific. She could only imagine the horror of losing a girlfriend at such a tender age. Then to become the prime suspect must've added insult to injury. What she knew from interviewing dozens of teens was that they carried a lot of guilt. They almost always found a way to blame themselves when tragedy struck.

The strong, virile cowboy next to her also seemed to carry the weight of the world on his shoulders even now. Fourteen years later.

Had the sheriff done the right thing accusing Dalton? One of the first rules of a murder investigation was to look at who was closest to the victim. She would need to know more about the case to make a better determination. For the sheriff to rule the death a suicide must've been a double blow, especially to someone Dalton's age at the time. "Maybe he'll get a hit on her cell phone and we'll have something more to go on."

She studied him. He would've been Clara's exact age. Everything had been so intense with her. It was one of the main reasons Leanne hadn't dropped everything to run to Cattle Barge when Clara first sounded the alarm. Leanne remembered the sense of urgency in her niece's voice and another wave of near-crippling guilt washed over her. Knowing she'd heard that same tone when Clara thought she might've done poorly on a test when she'd scored a B had normalized the emotion and made it seem like she was reading a cereal box instead of crying for help.

"In your experience, does this seem like the work of a serial killer to you?" Dalton asked and she didn't realize he'd been studying her for the past few minutes when she'd been inside her thoughts.

"There's a strong possibility but it's too early to tell. Contrary to how they're depicted on television, most serial killers have a cooling-off period in between murders. Fourteen years isn't too long for a second strike," she informed.

"Why didn't you hire your own investigators when your friend died?"

"Because being a Butler means I'm supposed to have money coming out of my ears?" His tone was defensive and his muscles chorded with tension.

"Sorry. I didn't mean—"

"The Mav wouldn't allow it. He said I should get back to work and forget it ever happened." Dalton paused for a beat. "I'm pretty sure he was angry that I didn't thank him for sending in his lawyer to get me off the hook. I never really knew if he believed I was innocent."

"The whole situation is a lot for a teenager to take in." She softened her voice even more. Being a detective, she was used to choosing her words carefully and using tone to manipulate the suspects she interviewed into giving more details than they'd planned or getting a confession out of them. Talking to Dalton, she wanted to take her investigator/interviewer hat off and be a woman. He'd been through so much, too much, really. No one should have to endure it, although she'd seen this and worse in her job so many times.

She admired the strength in the man sitting next to her.

Most people, her sister included, reached out to find pain relief in the wrong places and in turn piled more problems on top of a bad situation. Problems like addictions to drinking, narcotics or both. Chemicals were the express train out of pain that most people took.

Not this man.

And she respected him for it.

"There was no sign of a struggle in my niece's case. I'm guessing with your friend, too. That's partly why the sheriff is reluctant to call this a homicide. So, I'm wondering how this guy could manage to pull that off. I know my niece and she would fight if someone came at her," she said.

"Unless she knew him personally or he disarmed her in some way," he said with an apologetic look.

"You're right. Now that I really think about it, she would also help anyone in need. The person could've been familiar to her," she said. "I wonder who would know both victims fourteen years apart?"

"Good question." Dalton used his thumb to flip through pics, giving enough time to study details. Most of them were of the ground or the tree. "Off the top of my head, they went to the same school. Could be a bus driver or male teacher. Even an administrator."

"True. I wish I had access to her laptop. She

might've been communicating via email," she said on a sharp sigh.

"Maybe the link between them is location," he offered. "Alexandria and I were supposed to meet at the tree. How about you and Clara?"

"I expected to pick my niece up at her house," she admitted. "Although, she didn't like to be there more than she had to."

"Maybe she needed air." Dalton took a sip of coffee. "Could she have gone for a walk and ended up there? Where does Bethany live?"

"That's possible, but how much do you believe in coincidence? Even if I miraculously put them at the same tree fourteen years apart to the day and then suppose they both knew the person responsible, where's the struggle?"

"The first location might've been by accident but the second could've been chosen," he conjectured, thumbing another picture of the base of the tree.

"There are no marks going up the trunk to the branch." She pointed.

"With Alexandria," he thumbed another pic but didn't turn to look at her, "I assumed she was already knocked out and that's why she didn't put up a fight."

"There are drugs like ketamine that could've come into play," she offered and when he lifted a dark brow she added, "It can be crushed up and put in almost anything. It knocks them out and is easy enough to get."

"The date-rape drug?"

"Yes." She needed to ask this next question delicately. "Do you remember if the sheriff tested your friend to see if she'd been… *abused*…in any way?"

"No. Guess he didn't think he needed to," he said after a thoughtful pause.

"Meaning there were no indications of forced acts," she clarified.

"From the so-called interview, I found out that there were no signs of struggle, nothing under her fingernails, no marks on her arms. It's why the sheriff initially hauled me in. I was the last person who was supposed to have seen her alive and she had no marks or bruises to indicate she'd been in a fight," he said. "When they figured out that I was telling the truth, he shifted gears to suicide."

"Based on what else?"

"Alexandria had problems at home. Her parents weren't getting along. They were having marriage problems, serious financial problems, problems with her older brother. She wouldn't let me tell anyone. We'd been fighting about that and my drinking," he informed.

"The family was on the verge of losing everything. She could've believed it was her fault somehow." She brought her hand up to her face. "Stress could be a factor, but..."

He stared at her and she couldn't tell if he was looking at her or through her, but she already recognized that look he got when he had an idea. "What is it?"

"I was just thinking that suicide by hanging seems like something a guy would do," he said.

"You're right. Statistics put death by hanging as a far more common method of suicide for males than females. The latter usually rely on something less violent like taking too many pills. When they *are* violent, they normally take an object to their wrists. I'm glad you brought that up. That struck me as odd about these cases and I meant to mention it before." Everything had been moving so fast they'd barely had time to think.

"Which makes two in the same location, by two teenage girls, even less likely." He picked up his coffee mug but held it midair.

"Even so, if I look at this purely from an investigator's point of view, I walk up to a body hanging in the air, no sign of struggle. In your friend's case, I talk to a few people and find out that she was supposed to meet you, so you hit the top of my suspect list. Keep in mind the biggest threat to any woman is the person closest to her. Oftentimes that means we look hardest at the person the victim was in a relationship with. I'm guessing threatening you with charges was the sheriff's way of trying to get at the truth. I'm also assuming he believed it had most likely been a suicide from the onset. And if that's the case, he wouldn't truly have treated it as a murder investigation aside from trying to shake you down."

"Meaning?" Dalton asked, and he was following what she was saying with renewed intensity.

"There isn't going to be a whole lot of evidence that has been collected in either case, which will make it even more difficult to tie these two crimes together." She studied the picture of the tree trunk again, wishing it could speak. It held the answers, and there wasn't anything anyone could say or do to dig out the truth.

"Then we solve the current case," he said.

The waitress showed with the brown-rimmed coffee carafe and topped off their twin cups.

"Thank you," Leanne said as the waitress seemed to be waiting around for acknowledgment. The place was empty and she was most likely bored, Leanne thought, until Dalton glanced up and offered a polite smile.

The waitress's face flushed. "You're welcome. Anything else I can get for either of you?"

Leanne read the name tag. "No. We're fine. But thanks, Makayla."

Makayla lingered, like she was expecting Dalton to speak. When he didn't, she said, "Holler if you need anything else."

"We will," Leanne said, hearing the defensiveness in her own voice.

Makayla moved on and quickly disappeared behind the counter. Leanne shouldn't have cared one way or another if the waitress flirted with Dalton. But she did.

Her phone buzzed. She checked the screen. The call was coming in from her babysitter. Her heart stuttered.

"Excuse me while I take this," she muttered, scooting out of the booth as she answered on the second round of her ringtone.

"Everything okay?" she asked, skipping right over niceties, needing to know the answer. Her hands shook. Her blood pumped. And her internal alarms sounded.

"Fine here. How about on your end?" Mrs. Blankenship must've picked up on the stress in Leanne's voice.

"Sorry. I didn't mean to make you worry," she responded. "My niece's case is a bit more complicated than I'd expected. I'm most likely going to need to stick around for a few days. Is that a problem?"

Mrs. Blankenship lived on the same block as Leanne in Dallas. The grandmother of seven almost always had a grandchild being picked up or dropped off at her house and she always said how much she loved children. But Leanne didn't want to impose on her kind neighbor or overstay her generosity.

"No. Mila is just fine. She's been a little fussy. Might be getting in one of those teeth we've been talking about," Mrs. Blankenship said in her usual pleasant tone. She was the ideal image of a grandmother: white hair, generous stomach and gentle nature. That, and she loved to bake. If Leanne had had a grandmother, she would've wanted her to be like Mrs. Blankenship.

Mila loved her and she'd been a godsend when Leanne had returned to work, unable to drop her six-week-old baby—because that was all the leave she'd accrued—off with strangers at the day care she'd meticulously vetted. All it had taken for Mrs. Blankenship to offer her services was to see Leanne sitting on her porch step, cheeks and eyes soaked with tears while she held on to her baby in that little pink blanket when she was supposed to be back at work.

Mrs. Blankenship had taken the sleeping baby from her arms and told Leanne to go on. After a quick tutorial in her formula and feeding schedule, Leanne had handed over her daughter and a decent portion of her paycheck ever since. Her neighbor was worth every penny and more. Mrs. Blankenship was the rare neighbor who still baked cookies and personally delivered them on most major holidays. She had a knack for remembering birthdays, too. Every May 2, a card with a homemade treat was waiting for Leanne on top of the chair on her porch. The older woman had a quick smile and more energy than Leanne had ever seen. With her grandkids, she'd throw a ball or hop into the pool with them. Mila was lucky to be counted as one of her flock.

"I hate to impose with your grandkids coming over this weekend, but I might not be back until Monday," she said into the receiver, wishing her daughter was in her arms. "Can you hold on until then?"

"Don't worry. I just hope you find the person who did this," Mrs. Blankenship said in a hushed voice. It was the softest Leanne had ever heard the woman speak and there was so much sadness. Her husband of thirty-two years still held down his day job. Although, he had been threatening to retire for the past couple of years, according to his wife. Mrs. Blankenship had chuckled when she told Leanne. He'd taken an early pension from the force and worked as a security guard detail at a high-rise in Turtle

Creek. The man had no plans to retire, no matter how many times he'd said this year would be his last.

"Thank you, Mrs. B." It was the nickname the fifty-nine-year-old woman had asked to be called the first time they met. "This means a lot."

"Find the person who did this to her. She was a good kid." Mrs. B's voice started to break, but she seemed to quickly catch herself. She was one of the few people who understood law enforcement types.

"Give the baby a hug and a kiss for me?" Leanne asked, trying not to focus on just how much her heart ached at being away from her daughter this long. Other than an occasional late night on a case, this was the longest Leanne had been away from Mila. She'd underestimated how powerful that pull would be after going a full day without seeing her baby.

A grunt came through the line before Mila's unmistakable cry.

"She's waking up. I bet she's hungry. Be careful out there," Mrs. Blankenship said.

"You know I will."

Leanne ended the call and took a moment to breathe in the cool air outside. She turned and saw the waitress had wasted no time returning to the table. Why did a pang of—jealousy?—strike Leanne? She had no ties to the handsome cowboy and he certainly had none to her. The two of them were trying to solve a murder case, two actually, which reminded her that she needed to ask for his friend's file from fourteen years ago. Surely, there was some obvious link between these cases.

Makayla threw her head back as though cracking up at something the cowboy had said. Leanne's feet jutted forward and before she could say the words, *Back up*, she was standing next to the waitress and politely asking her to move so she could reclaim her seat.

Making a show of being put off by the request, the waitress blew out a breath and walked away from the table.

"Who were you talking to out there?" Dalton asked, picking up his phone and where they'd left off.

"The person who's taking care of my daughter while I'm here," she supplied.

"Everything all right?"

She nodded. "But I've been thinking about what you said."

Leanne pulled out a couple of twenties and tossed them on the table. Dalton sat there, a surprised look on his features.

"Take your money back. I already paid," he said, and she figured he was operating from some cowboy code, which meant arguing would do absolutely no good. He picked up the twenties and handed them to her.

"I'd ask you to at least let me leave the tip, but I'm guessing that's already taken care of, too," she said.

"It is," he confirmed.

"Well, if we want to figure out who murdered Clara we need to start with my sister." She issued a sharp breath. "Ready?"

Chapter Six

Dalton didn't pry in other people's business. He couldn't help but notice the strained relationship between the detective and her sister earlier. This visit should be interesting if she allowed them past the porch, which he doubted based on the way the pair had left things. Deception pushed people away from each other. It didn't matter how good the intentions might have been.

Several taps on the door to the small redbrick bungalow netted zero on the other side. It was well past noon and there was no sign of activity in the house. For all he knew, Bethany had taken her young child and disappeared. There was a chain-link fence around the property. The house sat on about a quarter of an acre of land if he had to guess. And there were no cars under the porte cochere.

Leanne knocked again, harder this time.

Just when he was about to urge Leanne to come back later, the door cracked open.

"Are you trying to wake Hampton?" Bethany spoke in the same quiet, angry tone May, the Butlers' longtime nanny and housekeeper, had used to keep young kids quiet in church. It was the one that said he'd be more than damned if he didn't get his act together. Bethany's eyes were dry. The tip of her nose was red, giving the impression she'd been crying earlier. She wore pajamas.

"Please let me in, Bethany. We need to talk," Leanne insisted.

"Why should I?" The fire in those words didn't reach Bethany's eyes.

"Because I want to find out who killed Clara and bring him to justice." Leanne's voice was composed, but a flood of anger stood like barking dogs behind a fence and threatened to unleash if her half sister didn't comply.

"You can't help with that."

"Don't be—" The door slammed shut in Leanne's face.

"Want me to give it a try?" Dalton figured he couldn't do much more damage than Leanne. Her sister might see him as neutral.

The detective stepped aside. "It can't hurt."

He rapped on the door of the modest house, using his knuckles. He'd need to take a lighter tactic than the bull-in-a-china-shop approach Leanne had used. "Mrs. Schmidt, this is Dalton

Butler. I'd appreciate it if you'd open the door and hear me out. Your daughter's case could be tied to one close to me and I'd very much like to find out if there's a connection."

She complied. But, again, she peeked through a small crack.

"Thank you for—"

"You were in the back of the car with us earlier," she cut in. "And at the sheriff's office."

"That's right. I couldn't be sorrier for your loss, ma'am." Every word was true and he could tell by her slightly softened expression that she sensed it. "I lost someone a few years ago in the same spot. Any chance you'll let us in and hear me out on this?"

"I don't know. Gary could be home any minute and he won't like the two of you here," she hedged, and there was a nervous twitch above her left eye.

Leanne took an impatient-sounding breath—the bull returning—so he touched her arm, ignoring the frissons of heat scorching his fingertips.

"We certainly wouldn't want to cause any problems between you and your husband, especially now while you have so much to deal with," Dalton said sympathetically.

His approach was working. He was gaining ground and he could see it. She shifted her weight from her left to right foot and chewed on her chapped bottom lip.

She swept the outside with her gaze, cracked the door open enough for them to slip through and said, "You can only stay for a few minutes. Hampton's sleeping and he doesn't know what's going on yet. If Gary sees your car out front, he'll freak out so make it quick."

All the honor codes that made Dalton the man he was, one who respected women and took it upon himself to protect anyone or anything smaller or weaker than him, flared up.

Was Gary physical with Bethany?

If he was, Dalton had to consider the possibility that he could've been involved in her daughter's murder.

Dalton followed the frail woman into the living room. He couldn't see into the kitchen with the boxy layout but a square dining table with four chairs, one with a booster seat that he presumed was for Hampton, filled the room. Based on the layout, he imagined the kitchen was to the left of the dining room.

A well-used sectional anchored the room with a matching ottoman that held several remote controls along with a few magazines. It was clear by the reading material that Gary owned guns. If Clara had been shot, the case might have been a no-brainer. Dalton filed the information in the back of his mind. It wasn't exactly unusual for a household to have a hunting rifle or shotgun in Texas. Most folks kept them for protection from animals.

But then again, the sickest animal in Cattle Barge seemed to be preying on teenage girls.

This conversation was going to be tricky in his estimation because Leanne, who seemed like a fine detective, was too emotional with her half sister to keep a clear mind. Her presence seemed to upset Bethany and that was another strike. The fact that her husband could come home any minute also seemed to put Bethany further on edge. Sure, he was a jerk but was he a murderer?

Dalton couldn't ignore the possibility that the man might've read about Alexandria in the news—maybe even found a reference Dalton didn't know about—and decided the time was right to get rid of the problem he had at home. Glancing at a picture on the fireplace of Gary with Bethany and Hampton said the guy had enough bulk to pull off carrying the teenager.

"You want coffee?" Bethany asked. "I just put on a fresh pot in case Gary came home."

Dalton picked up on the fact that she'd said *in case*. The woman didn't know when to expect her husband?

"If it's not too much trouble," he said as Leanne issued another sharp breath.

"None at all." Bethany's cheeks flushed. And then she looked at her half sister. "Leanne?"

Luckily, although to be fair Dalton didn't believe in luck, she'd kept quiet so far. She seemed to realize as much as he did that her talking would get them kicked to the curb quicker than she could find a penny at the bottom of her purse.

Seeing the relationship between these two helped him appreciate how close his own family was. The four kids who'd grown up together—Ella, himself, Dade and Cadence—had learned to band together early in life growing up with a father like Maverick Mike.

Their other two siblings who'd been kept secret until recently had been welcomed into the family and shown their rightful place as heirs. Not all of it had been easy, but he could see that it had been worth the extra effort on everyone's part as he watched Leanne and Bethany's relationship unravel under duress.

No matter what else happened, Butlers could be counted on to stick together.

"Yes, please," was all Leanne said. Good. Maybe she realized the importance of keeping her sister on an even keel.

The kitchen was where he thought it was,

around the corner from the attached dining room. The walls in this place were most likely thin, so he didn't speak. Instead, he moved to the fireplace mantel to get a better look at Gary. He was decent-sized, five feet eleven or so if Dalton had to guess. The guy had massive arms. He must lift weights and he had a tattoo running up one side that Dalton couldn't make out. He stood in front of something that looked a lot like a fishing cabin and he was holding his kid upside down by the boy's ankles. Gary didn't strike Dalton as someone who was rocking an overload of IQ points but this guy wouldn't care about quantum physics.

He was a trophy hunter based on the other shots on the mantel and the fact that a deer head hung over the brick, no doubt a prize buck from a hunting trip.

Leanne made eyes at him when he glanced at her.

"Wasn't sure how either of you took it," Bethany said, returning to the room holding out two fists of mugs and looking at Dalton.

"Black's fine for me," he said. Hadn't Leanne added sugar and cream to hers in the coffee shop? The fact that her sister didn't know said a lot about their lack of a relationship since reuniting. He didn't know much more about Leanne's past other than that she had a small child and no husband. That last part shouldn't have made his heart skip a beat as fast as it had. She was giving up precious little about herself and anytime he asked a personal question, she dodged giving a straight answer. He didn't think she was out to sabotage their working relationship, but she kept her vest buttoned all the way up. Which also made him not want to notice little things about her, like how she took her coffee.

Instead, he focused on the room, trying to memorize as much as he could about the place in case Gary showed up and cut their visit short. There were toys scattered around that obviously belonged to a little boy. Several pictures of Hampton hung on one wall, the fireplace covered another, and in the corner sat a fairly large flat screen television. There were no pictures of Clara.

"Sorry for the mess," Bethany said, bending down to pick up a couple of small cars before setting them on top of the ottoman. "Hampton just went down for his nap and I haven't had a chance to straighten up."

"That him?" Dalton pointed to the picture on the mantel.

"Yes. This picture was taken over the summer. Gary thought it would be a good idea to take Clara, so she and her brother could spend more time together."

"Don't you mean so she could watch him while Gary drank himself into a stupor?" Leanne said under her breath.

Thankfully, Bethany didn't seem to hear. She straightened up the magazines on the ottoman and lined the remotes next to each other until they looked like piano keys. An opened decorative box revealed a bottle of pills that he hadn't noticed before.

"I never did much decorating. Gary moved here first and sent for us once he was established," Bethany offered, as she held her hands out toward the dead buck mounted above the fireplace.

This must be her way of explaining why her home looked more like a hunting lodge than a place for a family. There were normally more feminine touches around when a woman lived in a house, in Dalton's experience, which also led him to believe that Gary was the one in charge.

"Sit down," Bethany said.

"Thanks for the coffee." Leanne gripped her mug but didn't take a sip.

"My Gary likes to take care of us so I don't have to worry," she said by way of explanation.

"Sounds like a decent man," Dalton said mainly to check her reaction. He took a seat near her and, now that Bethany was close, he could see that she'd taken whatever was in the medicine bottle.

He must've looked at the bottle a second too long because Bethany's eyes flew to it.

"Doctor likes me to keep these on hand to help me deal with…*things*," she said by way of explanation.

That gave him the impression the pills were some kind of antidepressant.

"Where's your husband?" he asked, figuring the question would come off better from him than Leanne. It was obvious to everyone, including Bethany, that her sister didn't care much for her spouse.

"He's probably out at the deer lease," she said with a shrug and awkward glance toward Leanne. "I couldn't reach him, which isn't unusual because cell coverage is spotty on a good day, and with the cold snaps we've had it gets even worse with all the wind."

If Gary was on the deer lease, someone would be able to corroborate his story.

"Who'd he go with?" Leanne's tone was sharp. She'd picked up on the same thing he had.

Bethany gave a noncommittal shrug. "I'm not sure."

"How do you know that's where he is?" Leanne asked outright. If he let her keep going, they'd be kicked out of there in a matter of minutes.

"What smells so good?" Dalton asked, trying to redirect the conversation.

Bethany's gaze bounced from her sister to him. "Cookies. I decided to make some for Hampton." She looked away when she said, "To soften the blow of what I have to tell him about his sister."

"Half sister," Leanne pointed out and that elicited a glare from Bethany.

He shot Leanne a severe look.

"Are those chocolate-chip?" he asked, trying to pull the attention back to him.

"Snickerdoodle," she responded. And then it seemed like the air staled and she had nothing else to say.

Dalton wasn't sure how far they could push her. She seemed fragile, like she was hanging on by a thread but also a little too quick to sweep the whole incident under the rug. Her reactions sent up warning flares about Gary. Did she believe he was as innocent as she said?

"Did Gary say when he'd be home?" Leanne asked.

"I'm not sure. I left messages. It's not unlike him to show up without calling me back first," she said, but something flashed behind her eyes. Fear? Dalton didn't comment on how strange the relationship seemed to him. If or when he was ready to commit to someone, he'd have the decency to let them know where he was and be sure he could be contacted in case of an emergency. If she knew who her husband was with, although he had to consider the possibility that she was protecting Gary and his friends, she was covering pretty damn well. Out of loyalty or fear? Or both? "Did you say there was another case?"

"Yes, I did," Dalton said. "Can you tell us anything about your daughter that might help us figure out if this case is connected to mine? Who were her friends?"

"She didn't have a lot of them. Gary said he wanted us to move before the end of the school year last year so she could make friends but that didn't happen," Bethany said. "She missed her friends back home and didn't even try to make new ones while she lived here. She kept threatening to leave, saying this friend or that had said their parents didn't mind if she finished school there, but Gary wanted her here with us where she belonged."

"What did you think?" Dalton asked, leaning forward.

Those bony shoulders of hers rose and fell again in another shrug.

"Who was I to stand in the way?" Bethany asked. "He was making an effort with her."

"What about being her mother and doing what was right for her?" Leanne ground out.

Dalton shot her another severe look but she seemed unfazed. She had a right to be angry. Hell, he'd wanted to fight the world after Alexandria's murder. But her attitude was putting Bethany on the defensive. Based on the tight grip Leanne had on the coffee mug, she knew it, too. It seemed to be taking all the strength she had to contain her anger. Even so, it was boiling over like an active volcano spewing hot lava all over their case.

He turned to Leanne and didn't speak until they locked gazes.

"Do you want to wait outside while I speak to your sister?"

"Half sister," Bethany clarified.

LEANNE GOT IT. She was blowing it. Dalton's message rang loud and clear. Get a grip or leave so he could finish what they'd come here to do. She shot her best look of apology and mouthed the words in case he didn't get the message. She really was sorry. Putting Bethany on edge—no matter how much she disliked Gary—would do nothing to help.

She chalked her anger up to Bethany not protecting Clara the way she should have. Bethany might be in a difficult situation with her current husband, but that was no excuse to allow him to make Clara miserable.

"Did she have any local friends that you knew of?" Dalton asked. "I grew up here so I might know the family."

"Other than Renee, I'm not sure. She was the only one who ever came over to the house," Bethany said.

"Why is that?" Leanne asked, using a much softer tone. In an interview, it was sometimes a good idea to throw a witness off by upsetting them. In this case, Leanne could see that her sister would just buckle and most likely kick them out.

"Gary didn't like strangers in the house," she said, looking to Dalton as though another man would obviously see the logic.

Dalton looked unmoved. "Renee Paltry?"

Bethany nodded after shooting a surprised look at him. She must've realized he'd know most of the families.

Leanne glanced at the medicine bottle and wondered if her sister was taking something on a regular basis. Clara had already said that Hampton was a handful when he was awake. A wild four-year-old was the least of her half sister's problems now. Because the sheriff would come after Gary and, at the very least, bring him in for questioning. Her brother-in-law wouldn't take kindly to having anyone poke around in his business.

Leanne wanted to march into Clara's room and gather evidence. Since she'd convinced the sheriff to look into the case, it would only be a matter of time before he sent a deputy to her niece's room. If Leanne's prints were all over the place, she'd be hauled in front of the Internal Affairs Division (IAD) to explain herself. Losing her job wasn't an option with a child to support by herself. So, she'd play it by the book.

"Did Clara have her cell phone on her?" The question was probably useless. Leanne had learned to ask them anyway. She never knew when an unexpected answer would break a case open.

"I believe so," Bethany said.

Leanne made a mental note to ask the sheriff about it. Her personal belongings would be released to the family unless he collected them as evidence. She'd left his office so abruptly earlier that she'd forgotten to ask. "I know this is hard but have you been inside her room?"

Bethany shook her head and tears welled. "The door's closed and I didn't have the heart to open it." She released a dry sob. Bethany had loved her daughter in the best way she knew how.

"What about her laptop? Is it normally in her room?" Leanne asked.

Before Bethany could answer, the back door smacked open, causing everyone to jump to their feet.

"What the hell's going on in my house, Bethany?" Gary's voice boomed from the other room as his boots smacked against the flooring. The floor groaned under his weight.

"You'll wake your son," Bethany said in a hushed tone.

"Whose SUV is parked out front?" Gary stalked around the corner and froze the second his gaze landed on Dalton. He must have known on instinct that he'd be no match for the cowboy whose head almost touched the ceiling.

Dalton's heft blocked Gary's view of Leanne.

"I'm afraid your wife has bad news." Dalton immediately repositioned himself so that he'd be in between Bethany and Gary. Leanne moved to her sister's side.

"I tried to call but couldn't reach you," Bethany said.

Gary looked the same as his photograph on the mantel, reasonably tall with a spare tire around his midsection and a ruddy face with pockmarks from too much acne as a teenager. Everything about him was big, from his big horse teeth to his big attitude. His mouth was big, too. Leanne sensed Dalton wasn't the type to put up with too much lip.

Bethany delivered the news about Clara.

Gary got quiet, listened.

"I'd like to speak to my wife in private," Gary said after a pause.

"Now, don't get upset, Gary. My sister is here to pay her respects and this is her new boy-friend." She glanced at Dalton, who supplied his name. "There's nothing going on and they were on their way out." Bethany stepped aside and pushed Leanne toward Gary. Leanne could feel her sister's hands trembling against her skin, a stark contrast to contact with Dalton. Leanne didn't correct her sister about Dalton being her boyfriend. Her sister had said it to calm Gary about another man being present.

A sinking feeling pounded her chest. Was he abusing Bethany? Clara?

Why would Clara cover that up when she spoke to her aunt?

Her niece had said she wanted—no, *needed*—to talk to Leanne about something. Was this it? Leanne had dismissed it as Clara becoming des-perate to get Leanne to pick her up. But physical abuse? Every time she'd asked Clara, her niece had denied it. But now the signs were obvious.

"I'm sorry for your loss, Gary," Leanne said, her tone laced with spite she hadn't intended. She didn't want her emotions to be transparent.

Her comment seemed to get him going, as his

ruddy complexion turned a few shades darker red. For a split second, she wondered if he knew what she was even talking about.

"You have no idea. I loved that girl," he said a little too defensively.

"I'm sure you did." She was goading him but getting a witness upset was an interview technique she'd employed many times in her career to catch someone in a slip. Besides, she could handle Gary.

"If you'd learned your place, maybe none of this would be happening. Did you ever think of that?" He fired the words like buckshot. They penetrated because she had in fact thought that exact thing. Leanne would eat one of her own bullets before she'd let him know just how accurate he'd been.

"I don't know, Gary. Why should I be the one to learn my place when you never did?"

Her brother-in-law's face took on a cartoon-quality expression. So much anger. Was he trying to throw blame on her to release his own guilt? Guilt at what, though?

Bethany jumped in front of Leanne, facing her, breaking her line of sight.

"You've done enough already. Go home, Leanne." Bethany's words were more plea than fight, and it broke Leanne's heart to hear the desperation in her sister's voice.

If Leanne had realized how bad the situation at home had become, not only would she have pulled Clara out sooner she would've gotten help for her sister, too. A little voice in the back of her head reminded her that she couldn't force anyone to do anything they didn't want to. It still stung and frustrated her to no end that she'd missed the signs.

"Get out of my house," Gary demanded, throwing his arms in the air and taking a threatening step toward Leanne and her sister.

Dalton had Gary pinned against the nearest wall before Gary could finish his sentence. His head banged against the drywall so hard a picture of Hampton flew off. The frame broke and the glass shattered as soon as it made contact with the floor.

"I'm going to tell you this once and you better remember it because if I have to come back, you're not going to like what's going to happen to you." Dalton used his forearm to press Gary against the wall. "Man to man, if I hear of you so much as grabbing your wife's arm too hard and leaving a mark, it'll be the last thing you do on this earth. Do you understand me?"

Gary's ruddy cheeks flamed brighter and he seemed to need air.

"I'm going to take a step back and you're going to apologize to the ladies in the room."

Dalton leaned forward like he was about to whisper in Gary's ear. Gary winced and Leanne could only guess that Dalton had increased pressure against his windpipe.

"Are you ready to show some respect?" Dalton asked loud enough for the women to hear.

Her brother-in-law's head was still turned to the side but he nodded almost imperceptibly.

"Okay. Nice and easy. And you apologize." Dalton must've eased some of the pressure because Gary gasped.

Leanne should have wiped the smirk off her face, but Gary had had this coming far too long for her not to enjoy it at least a little bit. And if he'd done anything to hurt her niece, Dalton pinning him to the wall for a few uncomfortable seconds would be the least of the man's problems. She'd have him arrested and throw the book at him herself.

"Sorry," came out on a rasp. Gary's hand came up to his throat where a red mark already streaked his neck. He carried the disposition of a child who'd been reprimanded. Bullies backed down the second they met their match. She'd seen it time and time again when the seemingly toughest men on the outside broke down, cried and begged to be released after a few days in prison.

Dalton pressed his hand to the small of Leanne's back and then guided her out the door. The move felt protective. Even though Leanne could hold her own in a confrontation, she liked the thought of letting someone else be in control for a change. It was nice for someone else to have her back when she'd felt so alone for most of her life.

Leanne barely closed the door of the sport utility when words exploded from her mouth. "He's hiding something and I don't like it. Where the hell's he been all this time?"

Dalton, the ever-cool cowboy, started the ignition and compressed his lips as he backed the vehicle off the parking pad and onto the street. "What was Gary's relationship like with Clara?"

"You've heard some of the stuff he pulled with her," she said, and a feeling deep in the pit of her stomach stirred. Call it intuition, but something was off.

"I don't mean any disrespect to her, but is there any chance there could be more to it than that?" He was talking slowly, choosing his words carefully and that sent up so many warning flares.

"Like what? A relationship beyond..." Leanne couldn't bring herself to say the rest. Acrid bile scorched her windpipe. She was shaking her head, praying there couldn't be any truth to his idea. "Not if she had anything to say about it."

"Hear me out for the sake of argument." His voice was a study in calm.

"Okay." Leanne took in a deep breath, meant to fortify her, but all it did was cause more acid to rise.

"He convinces her, possibly even threatens her, into entering into a relationship with him." He paused as though allowing her to take in what he was saying, like if he went too fast her head might explode. "Maybe she doesn't even like it, but she thinks he'll hurt her or her mother if she doesn't do what he says."

Leanne's chest tightened and it was getting difficult to take in air. Her mind couldn't even go there hypothetically. Her brain screamed *no*.

She listened for something to blow a hole in the story because it sounded like other horrific stories she'd known about.

"Maybe this goes on for a few days, weeks—" he paused another beat "—maybe longer. One day she freaks out. Says she can't keep doing this to her mother behind her back and threatens to come clean. He can't have that, so he kills her."

Chapter Seven

Leanne stared out the windshield. She brought her fingers up to the bridge of her nose as though trying to stem a headache. Dalton didn't like saying the words any more than she liked hearing them. But they had to discuss the situation.

"There are so many possibilities at play here. Aside from the fact that I think Clara would've told me something like that, I don't think it could've gone down that way. Let's just go down that road for a minute." Her mind seemed to be reeling at the thought of it happening right under her nose. "Say the two were in a…relationship. I know it would've been forced, because my niece couldn't stand Gary and I can't blame her. For argument's sake, what if he had threatened her mother and she gave in but she feels guilty about it. Eventually, the guilt eats her inside out and she tells him she can't do it anymore. He tries to convince her to keep quiet but she says she has to tell her mother. In the heat of the moment, he decides to silence her. A passion killing. He's hotheaded, so he'd use the first thing available. We already know he has guns but even if they were locked up, he'd grab the first thing available, a rock, a knife. Those heat-of-the-moment murders tend be ugly crime scenes."

Dalton wouldn't know from personal experience, but her points sounded solid. There were gun magazines and signs of hunting everywhere. In fact, Gary was supposed to have been out at the deer lease when Bethany couldn't reach him.

"Okay. How about this? Could he have seen the news coverage and decided to copycat?" he asked.

"He honestly doesn't strike me as someone who's bright enough to execute a plan as complicated as that," she admitted.

"I guess that theory doesn't quite match up with his quick temper," Dalton said, relief washing over him. He wouldn't rule Gary out, but he didn't want to believe the man in Clara's life who was supposed to protect her would hurt her. He turned the wheel onto the farm road 254. "We won't get anything else out of your sister now that he'll have a chance to work on her."

"You're right about that."

Leanne's cell buzzed. She fished it out of her purse and then checked the screen. "It's her." Her voice broke. "He better not have done anything to her."

Dalton pulled off the road and into the parking lot of a grocery store as Leanne took the call.

"What is it, Bethany? Are you okay?" There was silence but he could hear screaming through the receiver. "Calm down. I can't understand what you're saying." Leanne's forehead wrinkled in concentration, another little thing he didn't want to notice about her. "Start from the beginning and tell me everything that's happening."

Dalton drummed his fingers on the steering wheel. Whatever was going down was big and curiosity was getting the best of him.

"Okay. Here's what I want you to—" She paused and listened as though she'd been cut off midsentence. "No. There's no need for—" Another stop. "I'm going to break it down for—"

Leanne moved the phone a few inches from her ear. The sounds of her sister working herself into hysterics filled the cab. A kid screamed and wailed in the background.

"Don't do anything or go anywhere. We're on our way." Leanne ended the call and then looked at Dalton.

"We need to go back. I could barely understand what she was saying." The resignation in her voice had Dalton pulling away from the curb and making a U-turn.

"You didn't tell your sister to get a lawyer." He spoke his observation aloud.

"If Gary has nothing to do with this, he won't need one." Dalton could've guessed her answer. He'd thought the same, and it was the exact reason he wasn't offering up his family's attorney, Ed Staples. The man was the best in the state, probably the country, but he worked exclusively for the Butler family.

"The media is going to be all over this story once it breaks," he said. "Ever handle a high-profile case before?"

"Nothing that will get the kind of coverage this could draw," she admitted. She didn't have to say it but he knew—his name wasn't going to help keep this quiet.

The rest of the ride was spent churning over events. There was no preparing either one of them for the barrage of media already outside her sister's house, even though Dalton probably should have been used to it by now.

Dalton circled the block.

"This isn't good."

"These guys need something to put on the

air. Your sister seems…" He didn't want to insult Bethany.

"Fragile," Leanne said for him.

"She has a little boy depending on her, and I don't like what this could be doing to her mental state," he stated.

"Agreed. Hampton might be a pistol but he's just a kid. Clara's voice always softened when she talked about her little brother. I think she secretly wanted a big family. Lots of kids running around and to be the big sister to them all," Leanne sighed, and it seemed to catch her off guard that she'd done it.

Was that what she wanted?

Dalton was in no way ready for a wife and kids. Hell, he couldn't begin to sort out his tangled emotions when it came to his relationship with his father, let alone try to make a family of his own work. The Mav and his mother—who'd abandoned the family when his youngest sister was still in diapers—weren't exactly the best role models for making a marriage work. All the kids were dealing with the fallout.

"Any chance Bethany might agree to let my family's housekeeper take care of him until this whole situation settles? She could stay on at the ranch, too. It would give her a chance to grieve her daughter and not have to worry about cooking or taking care of a little one," he said.

"I don't have a lot of experience with kids but based on what I've seen when I'm out in public, those little guys can be a handful."

"You'd do that?" she asked, sounding a little caught off guard. "You'd offer up your own home to strangers?"

"If you think it'll help," he said. "And we're not exactly strangers anymore."

Most folks were surprised by the generosity of the Butler family, even though his sister Ella practically dedicated her life to serving the community through volunteer work. Ella fought to expand shelter space for stray animals. She worked tirelessly for the rights of the elders in their town. And yet, their reputation would always be that of their charismatic and unconventional father.

"I do. I just hope Bethany will be smart enough to take the help. When my sister breaks down, she tends to go inside herself and then use pharmaceuticals to equalize her moods. I can be hard on her sometimes, but she had it rough. We couldn't be more different, and I think that's part of the reason we ended up on opposite paths."

"How long do you think Gary will be held?" He circled the block once more before settling down the street where they could keep watch on the activity without being seen by reporters or deputies.

"Not long, if I had to guess. Sawmill must've found something on Clara's cell phone records that gave him enough to search the house. Gary was most likely brought in for routine questioning. The most they can hold him is seventy-two hours before they'll have to cut him loose," she said. "I'd call on favors to get more information from the sheriff but with the way this case is going, anyone at my department who's connected to me could end up hauled into IAD." She seemed to catch herself that he wouldn't know what those initials meant. "Internal Affairs Division," she explained.

Dalton admired the fact that she refused to put her colleagues—friends?—in the line of fire to get at the end she so badly wanted. He admired her sense of loyalty and respected the internal compass she possessed to keep her on the straight and narrow.

Her good qualities were racking up and he didn't want to notice or like any of them, dammit. And especially since the kiss they'd shared wound through his thoughts more times than he needed to allow. Tight-gripped control on his emotions had gotten him through some dark days during his childhood and in high school. And throughout his adult life.

"She's a mess. We need to go in before she comes out and does or says something she'll regret," Leanne said before taking in the kind of breath meant to fortify. She palmed her cell. "I'll let her know we're coming in the back way."

REPORTERS TEEMED ON the sidewalk outside. Entering through the back door, Leanne looked at her half sister. Bethany seemed so lost and alone, so small, as she paced from room to room.

Anger and frustration flared inside Leanne. She'd put away dozens of killers and predators in her time on the job, vowing to bring justice for those who couldn't speak for themselves. Why couldn't she make things right for her own family?

Locking away that unproductive thought, she squared off with Bethany, who was wearing a path in the linoleum floor, covering the kitchen with her pacing. Hampton was on her hip and already more than half the size of his tiny mother. Bethany's hair was disheveled and her cheeks streaked with tears. She was still in her pajamas and there was an opened beer on the counter.

The woman looked to be on the edge of a meltdown and none of this was good for the child on her hip, who was sniffling and rubbing his eyes.

"Can I hold him?" Leanne asked. She wasn't sure if her nephew would even come to her. She'd been so tied up with Mila and her job that she hadn't been out to see him in the past year. At his age, he'd most likely forgotten her.

Bethany looked to be holding on to the toddler for dear life as she shot a panicked look at Leanne. At least she wasn't yelling like she had been over the phone.

If Leanne had to guess, all the commotion coupled with his mother's over-the-top emotions had thrown him into quite a crying fit. Clara had said her little brother could throw a temper tantrum like a pro.

"I could take him to play in the living room. He won't be out of your sight," Leanne added. She'd read something about kids being able to pick up on their caretaker's energy and how, as such, their emotions could be impacted later in life if they experienced too much trauma. She could only pray that her daughter didn't feel the absence of her father. Dating her partner had been stupid, but she and Keith had been together almost all the time. If the department had found out, they would've been out of jobs. The one time she went against her better judgment and gave into emotion she let herself fall down that rabbit hole. Both had seemed to gain their senses quickly, breaking off the affair. Being partners became awkward after.

A few weeks later, the sickness came and she started throwing up every morning. Part of her must've known what was going on, even though she wouldn't—couldn't!—allow herself to consider pregnancy as a possibility. Their working relationship would be ruined. One of them would need to transfer, and she could've handled all that if Keith hadn't moved on and started dating a desk jockey. Then he was shot. Killed. And time had run out to tell him he was going to be a father.

Chin up, she was forced to pretend she had been in a relationship that had gone sour before it had gotten off its feet in order to save face for both of them.

Leanne refocused on her sister. Bethany's body was strung as tight as her emotions. Talking to her sister would require a balancing act and as long as Leanne could keep her own emotions out of it, she should be fine. She'd done this countless of times in interviews. Now shouldn't be an issue, she reminded herself. She rolled her head side to side, trying to diffuse some of the tension in her neck.

"You want to go with your auntie?" Bethany finally asked.

Hampton shook his head in a definite no.

The confident cowboy seemed to know the perfect time to step in. The big guy moved with athletic grace as he swooped down to pick up the nearest toy, some kind of cartoon character airplane, and then swirled it through the air. Seeing him be so charming with the tyke put a chink in the armor around her heart. She reasoned the reaction came from wishing Mila's father was around, not for Leanne's sake, but for her daughter's. Leanne hated that history was repeating itself given that her own father had never been around growing up. As much as she believed, preached, that people made their own destiny, she sure as heck hadn't seen that one coming when she'd started dating Keith. Granted, it wasn't his fault that her heart had broken after losing him, but the result was the same. All Mila had was her mother.

Hampton laughed despite huge tears welling in his eyes when Dalton dropped the plane low until it almost crashed against the floor. He made up a commentary about how the pilot saved the day and then popped back up, making the plane nearly collide with the ceiling in the small ranch-style house.

The little guy ate it up like spaghetti on his plate. He belly-laughed and Leanne marveled at kids' ability to be so in the moment they forgot everything—from tragedy to anger—in a manner of minutes.

She wished there was a toy shiny enough or that possessed enough magic to make her do that, too. She'd love to be able to shift gears and leave the past in the dust. Adults were so much more complicated.

And seeing Dalton Butler entertain her nephew was one of the most attractive sights she'd seen, even though she didn't want to see the handsome cowboy in that light. *Or any light*, her mind argued.

"Mr. Butler offered his family's ranch as a safe house for you and Hampton until all this attention dies down." Keeping her out of sight was one reason he'd made the offer. She kept to herself the part about wanting to separate her sister from Gary so he wouldn't influence her decision. And about needing Bethany to get off whatever pills she was taking to ease the pain of Clara's death.

Based on how hard Bethany was shaking her head this was going to be an uphill battle. "Gary won't like it when he comes home if we're not here."

This wasn't the time to try to talk some sense into her sister about the man she'd married. Leanne thought about Clara and about how much her niece had loved Hampton. For his sake, she needed to convince Bethany and not lose her cool.

"I understand," she started saying but Bethany cut her off.

"Do you?" Bethany drew her thin shaky hand to her forehead. "Because when all this blows over and it's just me and him, do you know what that'll be like for me? For us?"

"There are organizations that can help if you want to leave," Leanne said in as calm a voice as she could muster.

"Is that what you think I'm saying? I happen to love him and I don't want to go anywhere. Life has been good. Was good," her sister said, eyes brimming with tears.

"Really? Was it? Who was it good for? You? Clara?" Leanne couldn't help herself.

"That's not fair." Bethany released a sob and her eyes were wild, but Leanne could also see the fog starting to lift and a good dose of anger stir. Good. Because that was so much better than her sister being too numb to feel anything.

"I'm sorry about what happened." Leanne put so much emotion into those words. She was sorry. So sorry. Sorry that she'd let everyone down. "If I'd come sooner, maybe none of this would've happened." She meant it. She meant every word. Guilt was a relentless pit bull nipping at her heels.

Bethany dropped to her knees and put her head in her hands.

Leanne scooted beside her half sister and wrapped an arm around her. "I know how much you loved your daughter." Every word was absolutely true. Bethany had loved Clara as much as she was capable. It was part of the reason Clara had waited so long to ask her aunt for help according to her message. She didn't want to leave her mother and Hampton alone with Gary.

Gary was a bad husband, stepfather. But was he a murderer?

"Sheriff and his deputies took her laptop and her diaries," Bethany said. "What are they going to read about us?"

"Clara knew you loved her. I'm sure that comes across in all her communication," Leanne clarified.

"Will they take Hampton away?" she asked and her voice was weak again.

"For what, Bethany?" Didn't that get all of Leanne's warning flares going? "What are you keeping from me?"

Bethany didn't offer a response. She rubbed her still-red nose with a fistful of tissue she fished from her pocket. "I've already lost my little girl. I can't lose anyone else."

"Come with us to the ranch. Bring Hampton. You don't want to stay here alone until Gary is released. Not after everything that's happened." Leanne stood and opened the curtain to the front window. "Take a good look, because those people aren't going anywhere. Every time you leave the house, they're going to follow you and that could create a dangerous situation for Hampton."

Again, she was digging up everything in her arsenal to convince Bethany.

"What's Gary looking at? Honestly?" Bethany stared blankly at the wall.

"Depends on how questioning goes. I'm guessing he'll be detained for seventy-two hours. If they get anything out of him that they don't like, he's looking at a longer stay and a possible arrest." Leanne wanted to lie to her sister and make her think he would be in longer. But she couldn't. Not while looking at the fragile creature she'd become.

"That's three days."

"At a *minimum*," Leanne emphasized. There was a possibility that Sawmill might release him sooner if his alibi for the other night checked out. Being at the deer lease didn't exactly qualify unless one of his buddies could corroborate his story.

"Where's the deer lease?" she asked.

"Bonham." Bethany rubbed her raw nose again.

"That's what…about two or three hours from

here." Leanne performed a mental calculation. "Maybe three and a half if traffic is bad on the highway."

Bethany just shrugged.

"How long was he there?" Leanne asked. She'd rather be asking these questions somewhere else. Anywhere else than here, because there was a possibility that Gary could walk in that door at any moment. It was slim, almost nonexistent. But possible.

Bethany's cell phone rang. She darted to it like it was lifesaving water to douse a raging fire. "I don't recognize the number."

"If it's Gary, he's calling from a line at the station. He wouldn't be allowed to use his cell phone," Leanne advised.

A mix of hope and fear flashed in Bethany's eyes as she took the call. "Hello."

It must've been Gary because her shoulders fell slack for a split second.

"Okay." She ran to the kitchen and rummaged through a couple of drawers before locating a scrap of paper and a pen. "Okay. Got it." Bethany jotted down a note. "Why do you need someone like him?" She fell silent for a few beats. "I'll call right now."

Bethany ended the call.

"Who does he want you to call?" Leanne asked, splitting her attention between her sister and the handsome cowboy keeping her nephew entertained.

"A lawyer."

Leanne knew exactly what that meant.

Gary was under arrest.

Chapter Eight

Bethany's phone rang in her hand, startling her. She fumbled it before recovering and checking the screen. "Another unknown number."

"It's not him," Leanne said, and Dalton knew she was referring to Gary. "Let it roll into voice mail. Whoever it is can leave a message."

Her sister was close to agreeing to come with them, and Dalton figured that Leanne didn't want to lose momentum. He'd watched Leanne work on her, and it really was the best thing for Hampton and Bethany to get away for a few days. Leaving town immediately following his father's murder had done wonders for his state of mind. His eldest sister, Ella, had stayed on to manage ranch business until Dalton and Dade realized she was being targeted for murder. They'd flown home immediately and stayed at the ranch ever since.

The white-knuckle grip the woman had on the cell outlined her stress along with the deep grooves carved into her forehead and the brackets around her mouth. She seemed worn out and greatly aged, even though she wasn't more than a few years older than Leanne.

"Whoever it is, they're done." She held out the phone, showing that the voice-mail message icon had the number one written in the top left corner.

"Do you want me to check it for you?" Leanne offered.

"I'll put it on speaker." Bethany glanced toward her son. She turned the volume down so as not to draw Hampton's attention away from the airplane.

This is Carson Trigg with NewsWhenYouNeedIt! *I'd love to hear your side of the story.* He left a contact number before reminding her that she had an opportunity to speak on behalf of her daughter and help other families dealing with similar tragedies.

Dalton fisted his hands. Jerks like Carson who dug into other people's business in order to display their pain in public for ratings were some of the lowest bottom-feeders.

"It won't be long before all those people out there get your number and your phone won't stop ringing," Dalton warned.

As if on cue, her cell buzzed again. She

looked at it with a mix of fear and shock. "Unknown number."

"That's probably another one of those creeps who prey on other people's tragedies," he said with disdain.

"How do you know?" she asked.

"My father was Maverick Mike Butler."

"Oh." The word was so faint that he almost missed it.

And then the impact of his admission must've hit her full force because recognition dawned. Whether it was positive or negative remained to be seen, but he capitalized on the moment anyway.

"Hereford has the best security. You and Hampton would be safe on the ranch. Reporters wouldn't be able to get to you and there's plenty of help available so you can rest when you need to."

Leanne chimed in. "Hampton's a great boy but kids his age can be a handful. And you need time to catch your breath, process everything going on."

Bethany seemed to be considering it as her phone vibrated in her hand again.

"It might not hurt to have a little help. For Hampton's sake," Bethany said, and she seemed to be making up her mind. She shot a look at her sister. "I lost my temper with him for no reason a little while ago. He spilled juice on the kitchen floor and I snapped at him. Then I felt so bad we both sat on the floor and cried."

"You're under too much stress," Leanne said, and there was no denying the genuineness in her tone. She cared for her sister even if from an outsider's view their relationship was complicated. Hell, complicated relationships were a little too familiar to Dalton. He had no use to add to the list. But he would offer a hand-up to any decent person in need.

"How long do you think they'll keep him?" She was referring to Gary.

"I can't be certain until I speak to the sheriff. It's a long shot that I'll get much information given my connection to the case, but I might be able to get a few details out of him," Leanne admitted.

"The ranch is probably a good idea." Bethany exhaled and she looked exhausted.

"You need help packing a few things?" Leanne asked.

Her half sister shook her head as she pushed up to standing.

"Once we get her settled we can figure out our next move," Leanne said to Dalton. For reasons he didn't want to overanalyze, he wanted to make sure Leanne ate and had a chance to rest, too. Her sister wasn't the only one running on empty, and they still had a lot of road to cover if they were going to find out who killed Clara.

He told himself it would be good for the case if Leanne refueled, but there was something far more primal at work. He cared.

Dalton excused himself to make a couple of phone calls. He only needed two. One to his twin brother, Dade, who put the other siblings on conference as Dalton explained the situation. The other to the family's longtime housekeeper, May, to let her know what was going on and see if she could handle a few more mouths to feed. When she heard another child was coming to the ranch, she practically squealed. As he ended the second call, he realized he'd been white-knuckling his cell.

Frustration nipped at him.

The truth about what had happened to Alexandria felt like it was slipping away again with each passing minute. Answers that had felt so close hours ago were just out of reach.

What were they missing? They didn't have long to find out. He didn't have to be a detective to know the more time passed, the colder the evidence would get.

"You want to take a walk?" Dalton asked Leanne once her sister was settled in one of the guest suites in the main house. May was already doting on Hampton and the little boy was eating up the attention. Of course, it probably didn't hurt that she was the kind of person everyone wished they had for a grandmother. Case in point, she'd thrown a batch of her made-from-scratch chocolate-chip cookies into the oven the minute she found out a little guy was coming. She knew how to make the shorter set feel at home.

By the time they'd arrived, she had had the guest room ready to go, cookies coming out of the oven and had dug out some of Dalton's and his brother's old toys from storage. The woman was a force of nature and had been a surrogate mother to the four siblings who'd grown up under the same roof. The two siblings they'd gained since summer were getting their bearings and figuring out how they fit into the family. Accepting them had been easy. They were decent people despite having Maverick Mike Butler for a father. His absence from their lives growing up had most likely helped more than hurt them.

The one thing all six kids had in common was that no one had really known their father. Ella, Dade, Cadence and Dalton might've grown up with the man, but he'd stayed outside working the land and played his cards too close to his vest when he was alive. Ella had probably been the closest to their father. Several of the other children had made their peace with the Mav. Dalton wasn't sure how he fit into that puzzle. It was hard to resent a man who was dead. And yet, Dalton couldn't help but feel like their relationship was left unfinished.

The fact that the Mav's relationships were so complicated probably made it difficult for the sheriff to find his murderer.

"What could the sheriff have on Gary?" Dalton asked once he and Leanne were out of earshot of Bethany.

"If I had to venture a guess, I'm betting his alibi didn't pan out. Which means he wasn't where he said he was," Leanne said matter-of-factly. "It seems too soon for the sheriff to have any real evidence, but that would be enough to keep Gary in a holding cell for a while and let him sweat. He doesn't have a history of violent crime, but that doesn't mean he couldn't have escalated."

"We both know he's a jerk, but is he a murderer?" Dalton had his suspicions after talking it through with Leanne earlier. What if Clara had told her stepfather that she was moving to get away from him? Leanne had made a valid point about a heat-of-the-moment killing. But what if that wasn't the case? Could Gary be smarter than they'd given him credit for?

"That's the question," Leanne said, interrupting his heavy thoughts. "My professional instinct doesn't think so. I don't trust him, though."

"That last part's a safe bet." A selfish part of Dalton didn't want Gary to be the guilty party. There was no way the man had a connection to Alexandria fourteen years ago. He wasn't from the area and, as far as Dalton knew, never had been. Gary's age didn't match the age of the suspect to Dalton's thinking. Although, he couldn't rule out that a young person could be responsible for Alexandria's death, but it seemed more likely that it would be someone older. And that someone would be in his late thirties by now, early forties at most.

"If I had to guess I'd say Gary is seeing someone on the side and didn't want to give her name up," Leanne said. "My sister will be devastated, but I'm going to look into some programs for her. Get some referrals. From what Clara told me he isn't faithful. If Bethany can see it, she'll do what she should've done before—walk out on him."

"There should be a special place for men like Gary." Dalton flexed and released his fingers again. He wouldn't mind five minutes alone with the guy so he could see what it was like to fight his equal. But then, fighting Dalton wouldn't be a level playing field for the jerk. At six feet four inches, Dalton had a solid five inches on the guy and Gary's marshmallow for a spare-tire stomach had nothing on Dalton's athletic build. He came by it honestly, working the ranch.

With the physical labor he performed every day, there was no need for a gym membership and he'd been doing morning push-ups since he was old enough to have a patch of hair on his chest. The push-ups were as much of a habit as brushing his teeth. He could acknowledge that some of his rituals had come from needing to blow off steam. There was no better release than a quick morning workout followed by a long day on the land working the ranch.

Although, glancing at the curve of Leanne's hips, another thought came to mind as a way to work off stress. The thought was inappropriate. He chalked it up to too many nights without female companionship. Since everything he did made news, he'd been shying away from spending time with anyone out in public. Plus, he needed a little more than hot sex if he was going to spend time with someone. One-night stands hadn't interested him since he became old enough to buy a lottery ticket.

A relationship in the midst of all the chaos he'd been through was about as likely as a dust storm in Dallas. It could happen, but it would make news.

Don't get him wrong, he wasn't ready to trade his sport utility for a minivan and had never seen himself as the kind of man who would ever be behind that wheel. But the maturity that came with being old enough to grow hair on his chest also kept him from slipping under the covers with a woman without knowing more than her first name. All hot quickie sex did was ease a few tension knots. Real release accompanied interesting sex, and he had to be beyond courtesies with someone from the opposite sex for that to happen.

Leanne was studying him when he snapped out of his unproductive revelry. There was something about being back on his family's land, his home, that made him take stock in his life.

"What were you thinking about just then?" Leanne asked.

He wasn't ready to come clean and he'd never been much of a liar. "Things I shouldn't."

She looked him in the eyes and her honey-brown irises intensified as it seemed to dawn on her that his thoughts might've included her.

There was also something else he didn't want to see in those eyes—a familiar spark of excitement.

And then it dimmed like she'd turned a switch.

They stood there, neither of them moving as though at a stalemate.

It took a minute for her to speak but when she did, she'd recovered a cooler stare. "Maybe we should agree to keep a professional distance. It's best for the case if we don't get too…*personal* with each other."

"Done." It was true. Anything more than a working relationship was tempting fire based on his body's reaction to her so far.

She stood there, staring at him. Hesitation was written all over her features. And he almost made a stupid mistake when she dropped her gaze to his lips. She slicked her tongue across hers, and it took all his willpower not to reach for her and find out for himself just what she tasted like at this moment.

Drawing on all his considerable self-control, he turned away from her and looked out onto the land that had brought him so much peace. No matter what his relationship with the Mav had been, Dalton always felt settled on the land. *Until now.*

He chalked it up to old feelings being dredged up about Alexandria's case.

"What if I missed something?" Leanne asked, taking a step beside him. He could feel her feminine presence standing next to him and he could admit that it was nice. Maybe more than nice.

"Would Clara have come clean with you if you'd grilled her about her intentions?" he asked, needing a distraction.

"My experience interviewing people of all ages and from all walks of life has taught me that economic status, grades, none of that matters. When it came to teenagers, they were remarkably similar. All of them had secrets," she admitted.

"Makes sense," he said when he thought about it. "It's part of separating from parents, evolution. Plus, most of the people you interviewed had committed, were suspected off or had ties to criminal activity."

"When you put it like that, it's true. Most of the people I deal with have secrets."

"Which is a good point. What if Clara and Alexandria uncovered someone else's secret?" A picture was starting to emerge. One he didn't like but couldn't rule out. By the way Leanne's gaze narrowed, she couldn't, either. She compressed her lips, and that usually meant she was onto something. Now that he'd spent time with her, he was starting to pick up on her habits. Habits he probably shouldn't have allowed himself to notice.

"A secret worth killing for," she said. "Leads

me to believe there would be a trail. You know. I mean we have no real information from the past. It doesn't sound like the sheriff did much investigating with your friend's case and obviously, the trail froze up years ago. It'll be harder to make a correlation between the two."

"Maybe not. Doesn't it depend on what they had in common? I mean, when we find out what it is."

"How are we going to do that?" There was frustration mixed with exacerbation in her tone.

"Sawmill thought he had the right person. I was supposed to be the last person to have seen Alexandria alive. I was going through a rough patch personally and she'd threatened to break up with me if I didn't stop partying. Then, when I found out what happened I was in too much shock to say what I needed to. That I was innocent. I felt like it was my fault because of the problems we'd had," he admitted.

"And you still do," she said so quietly he almost didn't hear her over the wind. She shivered and rubbed her arms as though to warm them.

"What makes you say that?" he asked. She couldn't possibly know him well enough to read him, and he was certain he'd done a damn good job of stuffing his emotions down so deep that even he didn't think about them anymore.

"Because this situation with my niece is going

to haunt me for the rest of my life if I don't find out who killed her and bring him to justice. And even if I do, who knows if this weight will lift," she said in that same small voice.

"This is the first hope I've had in fourteen years that there could be a breakthrough in Alexandria's case. I haven't given life much thought past finding her killer." Was she telling him there was no escaping the demons? There had to be a way to put them to rest, because all his hopes were riding on finding out who killed Alexandria. If that didn't bring him peace, there was no hope. "Is it time to bring in a professional?"

"A professional investigator?" she asked.

"Why not?"

"I've thought about bringing in someone who could be more objective than me. We'll alienate the sheriff even more. Believe it or not, he's our best chance right now at getting at the truth. He has resources even a pro wouldn't have. Then there's my job. I have to consider the consequences if I get caught interfering with a murder investigation. I'll do whatever we can to find out on our own without stepping on the sheriff's toes. We don't want to end up hurting things when we're trying to help," she said after a thoughtful pause.

"We're facing the same problem with your case as I did with mine. The sheriff already ruled this a suicide in his mind. Even though he said he'd look into as a murder investigation his heart isn't in it," he said.

"On the surface, it's an easy assumption." Leanne compressed her lips. "But Sawmill arrested Gary and got a search warrant for my sister's house. He has something and he has a solid reputation. I asked around."

Dalton issued a disgusted grunt.

"He's learned from the mistakes he made early in his career," she admitted.

"I hope so. For all of our sakes."

Leanne opened her mouth to speak but his cell's ringtone rang out and she clamped her mouth shut instead.

"What's going on, Dade?" he asked his twin brother.

"I'm guessing you haven't seen the news coverage," Dade said and the ominous quality to his voice sent up a warning shot.

"What is it?" Dalton asked.

"Check your phone and then call me back. Let me know what help you need," Dade said before exchanging goodbyes.

Dalton pulled up the internet on his smartphone and thumbed through headlines reporting local news. Dread wrapped around him as he read.

"Dammit."

Chapter Nine

"The reporter?" Leanne asked, grabbing his wrist to reposition the phone so she could get a better view.

The picture was damning because the reporter was able to get enough of Leanne's face in it to identify her. The pair were caught in an embrace while standing underneath the tree where her niece had been murdered less than twelve hours prior to the picture being taken. Okay, this looked bad. From this photo, no one would buy the fact that this had been staged. The headline read, *Dallas Detective Brings Death to Cattle Barge*.

"First of all, I didn't *bring* anything and especially not *that*." She pointed at the word *Death* with a shaky finger.

Leanne would have a lot of explaining to do. First, to her sister who could interpret the entire situation wrong while under duress. Complicating their relationship further wasn't exactly on

Leanne's agenda, and her heart rate climbed thinking about the fallout. Dealing with the sheriff was going to be a whole other issue that raised her blood pressure up a few notches. There was no telling how he would look at this, and he could misconstrue her and Dalton's relationship and, worse yet, cut her completely out of the process.

And then there was her boss. She'd told him that she needed time off to be with family after losing her niece. How was this going to go over?

So, not only had this reporter violated her privacy but he'd done it in a way that could have her ending up in the unemployment line with no way to care for her daughter. Being fired from one law enforcement agency would make it impossible to get a job in another one due to civil service laws.

Even if that didn't happen, say that was the worst case, at the very least her credibility had just taken a huge hit. Her reputation was on the line.

Leanne felt sick.

"This jerk is going to sabotage the investigation and my career," she said, adding, "I need a minute to catch my breath." She took a few steps away from the handsome cowboy. She didn't need her superiors knowing that she was in Cattle Barge investigating in the first place, but how else could she explain herself? She'd worked long and hard to make detective before age thirty and she needed a steady career even more now that she had Mila. Being a single parent was difficult enough without being jobless to make matters worse.

Being with Dalton could hurt her own investigation, and his friend's case had gone so cold her fingers would become frostbitten if she touched the file—which, by the way, no one was going to let her do and especially not now.

She needed to perform damage control with her boss and with Sawmill. Where would she even start?

"I know what you're thinking." The low rumble of a voice came up from behind her, sending all kinds of inappropriate sensations skittering across her skin. He was close enough that she could hear him breathing and for a split second she wanted to lean back against his chest and absorb some of his raw masculine strength.

Instead, she turned around. Her body moved slower than she expected, as though turning too fast would overload her senses and she somehow sensed it on instinct. Breathing too much, too fast would only usher in more of his scent— raw, masculine. And all Dalton.

Leanne bit back a yawn, fighting against the tide of sleep that wanted to suck her out to sea and spin her around again and again until she gave in.

"You're not going to want to hear this but nothing else can be done tonight. You need a warm meal and a decent bed. We have both of those here at the ranch and I think it'd be best if you stayed over rather than risk reporters stalking you at a roadside motel." He was right. She needed all those things plus a shower and a toothbrush.

But how would she get her mind to stop spinning long enough for any of those normal things again? She'd let Clara down in the worst possible way. Doing something as menial and ordinary as eating seemed…selfish.

He was also right about sticking around the ranch. She wanted to make sure her sister was going to be all right and that someone was available to help with Hampton.

"Does that offer include a hot shower?" she asked, hoping she could clear the dense fog smothering her brain.

"It does." His blue eyes twinkled in the moonlight.

"Thank you for helping my sister. Part of me acknowledges that you aren't doing it for my benefit. You want answers and helping us figure out who killed Clara is a means to that end. We find Clara's killer and you might just be able to put your friend's case to rest. But something else makes me think your cowboy code would have you offering to help anyway. I appreciate everything you're doing for us and for my niece," she said. And she meant every word. No matter how confusing or upside down her life became, she was grateful to the handsome cowboy for everything he'd done and was doing. She knew that would also stop her from cutting him out of the investigation. He deserved to know the truth about Alexandria. It was the only way he'd be able to put his ghosts to rest and begin to think about letting go of the guilt that had obviously eaten at him for almost a decade and a half.

He nodded by way of acknowledgment. Something also told her he wouldn't let himself accept anyone's appreciation until he found the killer.

"Let's get a few hours of sleep and we can start fresh. We'll put our heads together and figure out a plan for damage control with the media. I'd like to include the family lawyer in that discussion. He's the best and knows how to spin a story in a better direction," he said. "Think Sawmill's finished with Gary yet?"

"Probably not. If he thinks my brother-in-law's involved in some way he'll keep him in the interview room all night if he has to," she clarified.

"Then you might wake up to find this nightmare is all over," he said, extending a hand to lead her toward the main house. "And you'll be able to pick up your life where you left off."

Was that something she even wanted anymore? Her life seemed somehow empty now. But that was silly, at best, to think being with Dalton for such a short time could alter her perspective.

Even at night she could tell the land was beautiful, and she could only imagine how much more enchanting it would be in spring when the bluebonnets were in bloom. But even in this setting she didn't believe in fairy-tale endings. Her niece was gone and her life would never be the same again.

Leanne had noticed the grandeur of the Butler home when she was getting her sister settled earlier. The house was a sight unto itself. It looked like something out of a resort brochure with its rustic charm and wood-beamed arched ceilings in the main room.

"I'll heat something in the kitchen," he said, hooking a left.

"Mind if I take a shower first?" she asked.

He gave her a once-over, which made her feel a little self-conscious before he said, "Hold that thought."

A few moments later, he returned with a woman trailing behind.

"Hi. I'm Ella. Dalton's—"

"Sister." Leanne nodded, smiled and shook the extended hand. Ella had a firm shake and an honest face.

She also had a bundle under her left arm, which she pulled out and held between them. "I wasn't sure about your size but I think we're close. These will be better than sleeping in your work clothes." Ella was a similar height and build to Leanne and that's where the similarities stopped. Ella had cornflower-blue eyes and bright red hair. Her complexion gave the impression she had some Irish in her.

Leanne had read about the elder Butler's involvement in charity work, and the woman was striking and seemed to be the genuine article, too. She took the offering. "Thank you."

"I don't want to keep you. I've been somewhat in your shoes and I know what it's like to finally get a hot shower," Ella said. "I'll just help Dalton in the kitchen. Make yourself at home."

"I can handle the kitchen," Dalton defended.

Ella rolled her eyes and laughed. "I was just trying to be helpful. Don't go all caveman on me."

Leanne laughed and it felt good. She'd become so used to seeing the dark side of life, it was refreshing to see something so basic as siblings teasing each other good-naturedly. Her relationship with her own sister was complicated. She held up the bundle, wishing her relationships were as easy as what she was seeing between the Butlers.

"And if you're so capable of domestic duties, why haven't you brought the tree home yet?" Ella teased.

Dalton shrugged, but Leanne saw something dark cross his features. Regret?

"Thanks, again," she said to Ella.

"Your room's this way," Dalton said with a half smile back at his sister. "I thought you'd want to be close to Bethany and Hampton."

"Your nephew is adorable." Ella's eyes looked like they'd been sprinkled with fairy dust. Leanne recognized that look. It seemed the older Butler sister wanted a baby.

"He's a handful but he's sweet." Leanne was embarrassed to admit how long it had been since she'd seen him. She'd been relying on Clara for updates. Bethany had made excuse after excuse as to why she couldn't come visit Leanne and the baby.

Leanne wondered how much the excuses had to do with Gary forcing his wife to stay home. Was he sealing her off from family in order to isolate her?

In order to hide what was going on at home?

THE SHADES WERE closed in the comfortably furnished guest room, blocking out the sun. Leanne stretched. Coffee. She needed caffeine.

It was 6:20 a.m.

There were no sounds coming from the room next door. Was it possible she'd woken before Hampton? Leanne never slept more than five consecutive hours since the baby came. Mila would sleep longer, but Leanne would wake to check on her daughter and make sure she was okay. Having a little girl had changed her in many wonderful ways. It had softened her and made her more sympathetic. It had also put her on guard 24/7.

And, it had also hardened her toward Bethany for her relationship with Clara. Babies were so small and vulnerable that Leanne couldn't imagine not moving mountains to protect them as they grew and especially after waking every few hours just to make sure her own daughter was comfortable and still breathing.

It was too early to call Mrs. B and check on Mila. She considered firing off a text to let her babysitter know that everything was fine and to respond when she had a few minutes to talk.

Leanne would wait until after she had a cup of coffee in her before trying to communicate with anyone. Her autocorrect had sent a few interesting messages before she was fully awake. Glancing at the clock again told her that Mila would be awake in another hour at the latest, but she'd need to be changed and fed right away.

Leanne sat at on the edge of the bed for a long moment, gathering her thoughts. Life moved fast, especially in her line of work. It was important to take a few minutes every day to slow down and breathe. A solution to a problem often came when she took the time to quiet her mind. She squeezed her eyes shut, wishing something would pop into her thoughts about Clara.

It had been thirty-six hours since her niece's body had been found. With every second that ticked by, the killer took another step away from the light.

Forcing a breakthrough wasn't working, so she pushed off the bed and headed into the adjacent bathroom. Her and Bethany's rooms were connected via a Jack-and-Jill bathroom so she tiptoed around, not wanting to disturb her sister. Leanne brushed her teeth, washed her face and then wandered down the hall toward the kitchen. The ranch-style layout had been easy enough to memorize. A fact she appreciated this morning with the fog engulfing her brain.

As she neared the great room, she heard voices. One of them belonged to Hampton.

"Good morning," she said to May.

"You're up early," May said, scooting her chair back from the table where she was playing cars with Hampton. "Did you get any sleep?"

"A surprising amount, actually. Thank you for having us," Leanne responded.

"You're no trouble at all. It's nice to have babies in the house again," she said, rising and moving toward the coffee machine. "I asked Dalton and he said you drink coffee."

"Yes, but please let me get it myself. You're already doing too much for us." Embarrassment heated Leanne's cheeks. She wasn't used to letting others do things for her.

"It's nothing." May waved her off.

"Really, I insist. It's the least I can do after you've shown so much hospitality." Leanne was by the woman's side, urging her to reclaim her seat at the table.

"Aunt Lee-Lee, look," Hampton said with a big smile. He pointed to a yellow car on the blue track. Even he was in a better mood today, and she wondered how much his mother's moods were affecting him. Kids were so good at picking up on emotions. And then there was this magnificent ranch. It would be hard to be in a bad mood waking up to this every morning.

"That's awesome, buddy," Leanne said, walking over to get a better look. He'd started calling her Lee-Lee when he was too young to say her whole name and it had stuck because Clara had encouraged it, thinking it was adorable. Leanne had to admit her niece had had a point. It was pretty stinkin' cute. She tousled his blond curls, thinking how much his eyes looked like his sister's, and said, "Good job."

May reclaimed her seat and Leanne poured a cup of fresh hot coffee.

"Dalton wanted me to tell you he's on the back porch," May said.

"I can take Hampton with me," Leanne said. Although, she half feared he'd cry the minute she tried to pull him away from his toys. And May. She had a calming presence that Leanne appreciated.

"Don't worry about us, right, Hampton?" The older woman handed him a red car.

"No way." He took the toy, rewarding May with another toothy ear-to-ear smile.

Leanne let a small sigh escape. This ranch had a magic she'd never known. A family magic that she'd never experienced with a mother who worked two jobs just to keep food on the table. Leanne and her mother had been close and she loved her mother. They had been more like sisters than parent and child. Her mother had done what was necessary to make ends meet.

The outside of the ranch was decorated to the nines for Christmas and the smell of fresh-baked bread filled the kitchen. The best thing about Christmas to Leanne's mother had been the extra seasonal jobs she could pick up so they could stay ahead of the bills. Leanne had worked from her earliest memories and the two had gotten by all right, combining funds to keep the lights on.

Her mother had kept a solid roof over their heads, clothes on their backs and food on the table. She was a practical woman who'd had no patience for emotions. Abigail West lived hard and took care of business. She never trusted men after Leanne's father had walked out despite bringing home several "uncles."

Her death had left a hole in Leanne's life, in her heart.

Life was hard. Kids were simple.

When she really thought about life, adults made it complicated. In her own case, she could acknowledge that her mother had never forgiven Leanne's father for walking out on her during her pregnancy. And, in little ways, she'd most likely blamed her daughter for their struggles, for how hard she'd had to work.

Her mother never would've said anything outright, save for the occasional outburst of angry words in the heat of the moment, which she later apologized for. She'd try to make it up to Leanne by making her favorite dessert. But Leanne had always known that she was the reason her mother had had a difficult life.

"Shout if you need help with him." Leanne wrapped lean fingers around the mug to warm them as she walked to the back door leading to an enclosed porch. Dalton was there. His long legs were stretched out in front of him. He stood the minute he heard the door creak.

"Morning," he said. "Come on out."

"Sorry. I didn't want to disturb you," she said. The screened-in porch was grand in scale, like everything at the ranch. There had to be half a dozen pairs of white rocking chairs. A small table with a checkerboard on top and two chairs nestled underneath sat on one side of the room.

The sun was rising in the east, not yet visible over the tree line, but casting a warm glow in that part of the sky. Dalton motioned for her to take the seat next to his. A small table was nestled in between.

"I was thinking about what we know so far," he said.

Taking her seat, she said, "I woke up thinking about it, too."

He shot her a glance that said he understood. It was a small gesture, really, but even so, it sent warmth circulating through her.

"Going over the sheriff's initial assessment, I can't make sense of his line of thinking. Christmas break is almost here. Clara would have gotten time off from school. Why would she commit suicide now?" he asked.

"Exactly."

"She and her stepdad didn't get along." Dalton restated what they already knew.

"Not a bit." She took a sip of the steaming brew. "I can admit that she wasn't in a good place about a lot of things. She missed her friends in San Antonio. She didn't feel like she fit in here in such a small town with nothing to do besides help her mother and work at the whim of her stepfather."

"We know she wasn't making new friends here in Cattle Barge. What about a boyfriend?" he asked.

"His name is Christian," she said. "And he lives in San Antonio."

"Have you spoken to him?"

"Not since this all started. No." She took a sip of fresh brew.

"How long have they been together?" His

forehead creased and she realized why he'd be concerned about the boyfriend.

"A year, I think. At least, she told me about him last Christmas and I got the impression it was a new thing," she detailed. "He works three mornings a week plus weekends in a bagel shop in order to save money for college, going in at four o'clock in the morning before school. From everything Clara said about him, he's a good guy."

"He shouldn't find out something like this about his girlfriend on the news." His deep voice was low and his jaw clenched. There was so much pain. "If they're like every other young couple, he's already worried that she isn't answering his texts."

Having gone through something similar, Dalton would know what to say. Leanne drew a blank, which wasn't normally an issue for her but this wasn't an ordinary situation. She was too personally involved and shutting out her feelings—again, something she'd learned to do in order to survive—wasn't an option. She felt for Christian. "We'll make the call in a few hours when he wakes up."

"I can talk to him."

"That would be nice," she offered.

"What else do you know about her home

life?" he asked, refocusing toward the landscape beyond the screen.

"Gary's punishments were becoming worse. That's why she wanted to stay with me. She needed to escape and figured he would cool down if she was gone for a while," she admitted with that now-familiar guilt.

"It's not uncommon for teenagers to rebel," he offered.

"I'm not saying my niece was perfect by any means. I've heard her snap at her mom. But she wanted her mom to be happy and for Hampton to have both of his parents in the home. She tried to get along with Gary and not create any friction, and I think she felt like it was her fault they didn't click."

"Kids have a way of blaming themselves for everything." He paused for a couple of beats. "Which is another reason it's important for us to speak to Christian. He'll walk around the rest of his life with the guilt that he didn't realize what was going on and help her."

Based on what she knew about Dalton so far, he most likely fell into that same category. Would he ever be able to let go of the guilt that caused dark circles to cradle his too-serious-for-his-age blue eyes?

It struck her that while most people their ages were settled down and well into establishing their own families, she and Dalton were single and grieving. She had Mila and that was the beginning of more of a home life. Before the baby, all Leanne did was work and eat out. She didn't cook, not that that was a requirement, especially since she worked. But wasn't it a little odd that she couldn't melt butter on a stove if she had to?

Did it even matter? Would Mila notice? Or would her daughter have a similar childhood as her mother? The thought hit deep. By twelve, it wasn't uncommon for Leanne to stay in the apartment alone overnight while her mother spent time with an "uncle" when most kids her age were having sleepovers.

Last night, when she'd pulled the covers over her, she went to sleep thinking about Dalton's easy relationship with his sister and what growing up in a supportive family might feel like.

There was something intimate about sitting on the porch with Dalton, being able to read some of his thoughts.

The kiss they'd shared, their embrace, trickled into her thoughts, too. She'd felt something stir when she'd been in his arms, and it was something that had been absent in physical contact with all her past relationships combined... *chemistry*?

With Keith, sex had been more about being

together so much they'd felt like a couple. They'd had a similar sense of humor and work schedule.

Speaking of which, she wondered how she'd ever put the pieces of her life back together. The past couple of days had felt like an out-of-control Ferris wheel, spinning and churning. And nothing would ever be the same without her niece.

There was no room in her life for a man, no matter how much her body wanted to feel Dalton's on top of her, blanketing her with his athletic frame.

Talk about lost causes. This man was haunted by a ghost from his past. Even if they decided to date—and that was a ridiculous notion for more than just logistical reasons—how could she ever compete with the memory of the girl from his past?

She didn't even want to try. The two of them had been together when they were barely more than kids; life was about what to wear to prom. It was all promise and young love. Pure. Nothing was complicated.

Dalton had hinted at a difficult relationship with his father but Leanne couldn't imagine that it could've been too difficult, considering he grew up in a warm place like this with siblings around. She could already see that his and Ella's relationship was special.

Leanne knew nothing about siblings. She hadn't even known about her sister until she'd turned sixteen and her mother sat her down and told her. It had taken another half a dozen years to decide to track Bethany down.

Leanne's cell buzzed, breaking through her revelry.

She fished it out of her pocket, looked at the screen and gasped.

"It's Gary."

Chapter Ten

"Hello?" A beat passed and Leanne's body tensed. Her face muscles pulled taut, tension written in the lines of her forehead. "I'm not telling you where she is, Gary."

He'd made his one mandatory phone call last night. Unless Dalton was missing something, the man must've been released.

"She doesn't have her phone right now." Leanne's voice was a study in simmering anger.

Dalton sipped his coffee, listening to one side of the conversation.

"No, I won't go get her. I didn't say we were in the same place," she said tersely. And then seemed to realize she might be making things worse for her sister when she added, "She just lost her daughter. She needs a little time. Surely, you can underst—"

He must've cut her off and said something to offend her because her shoulders flew back and her posture became rigid.

"I'm sorry if you can't understand what's happening. All I can tell you is that she's safe and—"

Leanne blew out a frustrated-sounding breath. "No, the best place for her isn't home." She paused. "The reporters are one thing—" Another beat passed. "Maybe if you'd listen instead of flying off—"

She set her phone down in her lap. Dalton could hear the yelling even though the words were difficult to make out.

After taking a sip of her coffee, she picked up the phone. "You do realize that you just threatened a law enforcement officer. That's a felony offense in case you were unclear, and I won't care who you're married to when I file a complaint against you."

Now the line was quiet.

"Not exactly your brightest move, considering you're still under suspicion for my niece's murder. And I will testify against you to get the truth, Gary. Harass my sister and I'll haul you in myself," she bit out. "If you ever hurt her again, you won't make it that far."

Gary seemed to be taking in that last comment based on the silence that followed. That was the funny thing about bullies. They usually knew when they'd met their match and it didn't take long to buckle. Dalton felt nothing but pride for Leanne standing up for her sister, for herself. His chest swelled with it.

Leanne ended the call and looked at Dalton with defeat. "She might not be answering now because she's asleep, but the minute she realizes he's out, she'll go home."

"Maybe not."

"Past behavior is always the best predictor. She always jumps as soon as he snaps his fingers. That's what Clara told me," she said.

"I wish they'd held him longer, given us more time." He couldn't argue her point, so he didn't. But he hoped recent events had caused Bethany to rethink her home situation. And maybe make a better choice moving forward.

"Seventy-two hours was the maximum. I'm not surprised he's out. We should speak to the sheriff and do some damage control," she said and he agreed.

She pulled up his direct line on her smartphone, tapped the name and then put the call on speaker.

"I have Dalton Butler here and he's on the call with us," she informed the sheriff after the perfunctory greetings.

"Dalton," the sheriff said by way of acknowledgment. It was short and his voice was tight, signaling he wasn't thrilled with the photo of the two of them from the parking lot the other morning.

"Morning, Sheriff."

"Sir, you released Gary Schmidt this morning," she began.

"My office has a strict policy of not commenting publicly on an ongoing investigation," Sawmill said in that matter-of-fact voice Dalton had heard used before with the media.

"I understand your position but I'm not a run-of-the-mill citizen or media outlet," she defended.

"That may be. However, I'd advise you to call your supervisor if you want more details. I agreed to release information to him in my report as a professional courtesy, which I'll have to him later this morning." Dalton had also heard that tone before. This issue was done. Over. Applying more pressure wouldn't help.

"Will you at least tell me how you're classifying this case?" Tension lines creased her forehead as she brought her hand up to cup it.

"I'm not at liberty to discuss the details with you." She seemed to realize at the same time he did that Bethany was most likely the only one who could get more information. Even that was questionable, considering her husband had been interviewed as a possible suspect.

Talking to Sawmill was as productive as trying to climb a wall wearing mittens.

"Can you tell me if my niece was violated?"

He stalled for a long moment and Dalton figured he was debating with himself about telling her. On the one hand, Leanne had a right to know if her niece had been assaulted.

The sheriff finally said, "She was not."

"Thank you for your time, sir," Leanne said before ending the call and turning to Dalton. He could see the relief moving behind her honey-brown eyes.

"That boyfriend of Clara's. Any chance he's up and working a shift at the bagel shop today?"

"It's possible." She glanced at the clock on her phone.

"San Antonio isn't that far of a drive." He leaned forward, resting his elbows on his knees. "I'd like to be there in person. See his reaction to the news about Clara."

"You don't think he's involved, do you?"

"No."

"I'll get dressed." She stood and then hesitated before entering the house. "I leave Bethany here and she'll be out the door the second her eyes open."

"That's highly possible." He rose to his feet. "But we have other problems to deal with right now."

LEANNE FEARED THE minute she walked out the front door her sister would wake up, see the messages from Gary and run right back to him. That line of thinking almost had her canceling the visit to see Christian.

There were no guarantees that Bethany would stick around, even if Leanne stayed inside the house and waited for her to rouse. She could wake her sister up. But, again, that wouldn't do any good once Bethany heard one of Gary's messages. She must've turned off her phone or she would've already been gone. But then, she'd assumed that Gary was going to be in jail for a few days.

There was no telling how Bethany would react to finding out he'd been released. But Leanne was pretty sure this was the last time she would see her sister. Gary would never allow the two to communicate again after the way she'd threatened him and with Clara out of the picture, there was less of a reason to. Gary would never allow Leanne to be as close to Hampton.

With a deep sigh, she brushed her hair and pulled it off her face into a ponytail before dressing in jeans that were a size too big. She belted them and put on the shirt, grateful her undergarments had been washed and folded and were waiting on the bed. Then, she put on her shoulder holster and covered it with her blazer.

Before leaving, she cracked the door to her sister's room and peeked inside. Bethany's slow, even breathing said she was still asleep. A peaceful sleep? Not with the way her covers were bunched around her, making it look like a tornado had blown over the bed and somehow missed everything else in the room.

She prayed recent events wouldn't overwhelm her sister, causing her to slide into old patterns. Hampton needed his mother. And, dammit, Leanne needed a sister. Losing her mother and being faced with having no family ties left had been the reason Leanne had tracked her half sister down in the first place.

Bethany had been teetering on the edge when Leanne located her. Leanne found a rehab facility that she could afford and threw her energy into finding parenting classes for her sister. She'd gone to a few with her just to ensure Bethany showed up. Despite growing up in difficult circumstances, Clara had been such a bright light. Her life had been filled with so much promise.

It wasn't an easy road but Clara had been thriving in San Antonio. She and her mother had been on a good path when Bethany met Gary. The unexpected pregnancy threw in a few wrinkles but Gary came off like he was happy about it. He seemed to make an attempt to have a relationship with Clara by driving her to school every morning on his way to work. Everything had seemed fine on the surface.

Until he'd lost his job and started drinking.

Clara had protected the situation when Leanne first noticed the changes and asked about them. Her niece had defended his actions, saying she thought it was better if she caught a ride to school with a friend instead of getting a ride with him, so he would have more time to look for a job. She'd had a solid group of friends in San Antonio where she'd grown up. It was one of the reasons Clara had wanted to stay home—and, in hindsight, why Clara had covered her stepfather's actions—when Leanne asked about their home life.

Leanne could be honest enough to admit that Clara was known to keep a secret if she thought sharing would hurt the other person or upset the applecart too much. *I should've listened. I should've taken you more seriously, Clara.*

Kicking herself again wouldn't do any good. She knew that on some level. And yet, she'd never forgive herself. What if she'd gone to pick up her niece a week earlier? If Dalton was right, the date was important.

Bethany took in a deep breath, popped her head up off the pillow and then resettled almost immediately. Leanne froze.

When she was certain her half sister was

asleep again, she slowly shut the door and tip-toed down the hallway until she was far enough away to exhale.

Would San Antonio give her the answers she craved? Or, like everything else, would it cost more valuable time?

"I KEEP RUNNING around in circles in my mind trying to figure out if he's involved," Leanne said, after spending a half hour in companionable silence.

"I've been thinking that we should let the sheriff take care of the obvious," Dalton said, adding, "Maybe we should focus on the ways the girls might've been linked."

"That's a good strategy. I'm getting nowhere without being able to access the evidence and the sheriff isn't going to cooperate, so it's all speculation on my part." He was right. She needed to move on to what she could control instead of stressing about what she couldn't. The sheriff would be covering traditional bases. She had to assume he'd found something or he wouldn't have been able to detain Gary. Releasing him this quickly could mean his alibi had held up, at least for now. Concentrating their efforts on the road less traveled was a good strategy. It could also keep them from bumping heads with Sawmill. They'd already brainstormed a few possible connections, so she took out a notepad and scribbled them down.

"We could start at Cattle Barge High School. See if they had any of the same teachers," he offered. "Think your sister would give you her schedule?"

"It would be easier than trying to go behind her back and get it from the school," she said. "We might even get her full cooperation if we tell her that we're trying to find someone besides Gary to name as a suspect."

"Worth a shot," he agreed, pulling off the highway. "There's another angle we owe it to ourselves to consider."

"And that is?"

"It's possible that someone could be using this situation to get at me." His words were heavy, and she could tell he'd been carrying around the guilt associated with the possibility. "I've read everything I could get my hands on that's been reported about Alexandria. The sheriff is right. Reporters drudged up details of the past after my father was killed. I'd been avoiding the reports but stayed up last night reading everything I could find."

That explained the dark circles cradling his eyes today and the reason he'd rubbed them several times on the ride over.

"If we're going to consider this," she began

carefully. It was obvious the possibility was agonizing for him, even though he'd never admit how deeply it seemed to cut. "We could also say that someone could be trying to rattle you. To get at you or throw you off balance. With your father's recent murder, someone could be trying to get revenge on the family."

Was Clara an innocent victim in a plot aimed to make the Butler family suffer?

"My father lived an exaggerated life. He did things none of us are proud of. I'm sure he had a long list of enemies," he admitted.

"But why would someone specifically target you?" she asked. "With all due respect, he's already gone."

A revenge-against-his-father plot didn't work for that exact reason. Why target someone's child when the person was gone and therefore wouldn't be around to see it?

"True. I still think we need to put it on the table for consideration." She could tell that he was committed to finding the truth, even if it cost him something precious—the answer to what really happened to Alexandria. Because if this was some sort of revenge killing, that meant Alexandria's murderer might never be brought to justice. And he'd been waiting fourteen years so far to figure it out.

"Okay, then we have to consider motive. It's

murder investigation 101. Who stands to gain from tipping you off balance? Why wouldn't they just go after you?" she asked.

"Maybe they want me to be distracted so they can go after something on the ranch," he threw out there.

It didn't stick.

"You have how many siblings and staff working there every day, day in and day out?" she asked.

He started rattling off names. She waited a few seconds before politely interrupting him.

"That's a whole lot of people. If you're distracted, the ranch still runs just fine. Am I right?"

He nodded.

"So we can probably rule that out as a motive." She thought for a long moment about non-Gary possibilities. "Have you kept in touch with Alexandria's family?"

"I'm pretty much the last person they want to see," he admitted tersely.

"Did she have any siblings?" she prodded. Based on the increased tension in his posture he was still uncomfortable discussing details of her life.

"She was the youngest of three kids. Her brothers were a few years older than us and a year apart from each other." He followed GPS onto a side road as buildings came closer together. Traffic had noticeably thickened as he made a right onto a road that promised to take them into the suburbs.

"Did her parents ever divorce?" she asked.

"Took another six months, but they did. Mrs. Miller stayed in Cattle Barge but her husband moved years ago. I think to Houston."

"I could reach out to them. See what they're up to now." She wasn't sure if it would net anything, but it wouldn't hurt to make a couple of calls.

The voice on his GPS interrupted her, telling him they'd arrived at their destination. There was a strip shopping center on the left, so he pulled into it.

Leanne scanned the storefronts for the eatery. "There."

"Got it," Dalton said, cutting the wheel right. He seemed to zero in on the place because he was parked a few seconds later. He took a deep breath before exiting the vehicle to meet her in front of his sport utility. "Will he recognize you?"

"I'm sure Clara sent a picture of us. You know how kids are with their cell phones these days," she said.

"Good. We won't have to waste time explaining who you are or gaining his trust," he said.

"I'll handle his supervisor," she said as they walked toward the door. She dreaded this part. Having to tell someone a person they cared about was gone. It hit twice as hard since it was Clara.

First, she'd have to speak to his supervisor. Leanne reached inside her purse and dug around for her badge. The conversation would flow better if Christian's boss saw her credentials first.

A short woman in her early forties with dark hair greeted them from behind the cash register. "How can I help you?"

"I'm Detective West," Leanne flashed the badge in her palm, "and this is my associate, Dalton Butler." Leanne worried his last name would garner a reaction but the woman seemed to fixate on the badge instead. It was a common reaction when a detective showed up out of the blue in someone's life. Their next move was to check for a gun. Hers was tucked in her shoulder holster underneath her navy blazer that she'd thrown on over the borrowed shirt from Ella.

Her gaze searched for the weapon. Found it.

"I'm looking for the manager," Leanne said.

"She's right here." The woman gestured toward herself by sweeping her hand in front of her body. She had the build of a seasoned baker, full and round. Everything was short about the woman, her haircut, her height and her fingers. Dark circles cradled her eyes.

Leanne glanced around. "Can I speak to you for a moment privately?"

"Am I in some kind of trouble?" The woman's light brown eyes widened.

"No. Nothing like that. I have a sensitive matter to discuss with one of your employees," she reassured.

"Christian?"

"How'd you know?" Leanne asked.

"He's the only one here right now," the woman said as he emerged from the kitchen, holding a fresh tray of bagels for the counter display case.

He glanced from Leanne to his boss and then to Dalton, seeming to take the whole scene in. "What's going on?"

At seventeen, he was tall for his age, a little more than six feet, and hadn't filled out in the chest yet. He was a good-looking, hardworking kid and Leanne hated the news she was about to deliver.

"Let's talk a walk," Leanne said, motioning toward the door.

Christian's gaze followed her hand and then

snapped to his boss for approval. He had a suspicious, lost look in his brown eyes.

"Go on," the woman urged. She seemed to catch on that he was about to get terrible news or maybe she was trying to score some brownie points with a detective when she added, "Take all the time you need. I'll leave you clocked in."

Either way, Leanne appreciated the goodwill.

The three of them walked out front as a blast of wind knocked the door out of Dalton's hand. He righted it and then secured it closed.

"You're Clara's aunt." It was a statement. "What are you doing here?"

"We came to talk to you about Clara," Dalton said. His low rumble of a voice held so much compassion. He put his hand on the guy's shoulder, and the move seemed to calm Christian's nerves. His breathing was shallow and his complexion was already starting to pale. He knew this was going to be bad. But she could tell that he had no idea just how bad it was about to be.

"I've been trying to get a hold of Clara like crazy after a sheriff called and asked where I was the other night. She hasn't been returning my calls or texts," he said, his voice rising at the end like he knew something was wrong. "I figured her stepdad—" he glanced at Leanne and then Dalton "—she called him Gare-the-grumpy-bear. Well, anyway, I thought maybe he took away her phone once he found out."

Found out about what?

Chapter Eleven

"Where is she? What happened? She's okay, right?" Christian started firing off words, sounding more desperate with each question. His gaze darted from Leanne to Dalton.

Leanne would circle back around to his comment once Dalton filled the kid in.

Dalton looked the young man directly in the eyes. "She got involved with someone who took her life."

Dalton paused as Christian sucked in a burst of air. Tears welled as his gaze bounced from Dalton to Leanne and back in sheer disbelief.

His legs seemed to give but Dalton held him upright with a strong hand on his arm. "This is my fault. I should've told—"

"I'm going to stop you right there, son. There was nothing you could've done to save her," he reassured, walking him over to one of the chairs on the small patio area.

Christian sat down, his expression stunned. "Are you sure it was her?"

A quick nod confirmed the worst.

"This can't be happening." His face paled as shock kicked in. "I just saw her last week."

"Did she talk about meeting someone new or making a new friend?" Leanne asked, taking the seat opposite Christian.

"No. She couldn't stand anyone where she moved." He looked up with wet brown eyes. "That's why she wanted to kick it at your place for a while."

"Had she and Gary been in a fight?" she asked, needing to know if she could rule him out.

"Which time?" He sucked in another burst of air. "You don't think it was him, do you? He started getting rough with her mother after the move."

Based on his shocked expression, Christian was having a difficult time processing this news, as expected. It was clear that he cared a great deal for Clara.

"Hitting her?" Leanne braced for the answer.

"Grabbing her by the arms and leaving bruises." Fire glinted behind his eyes. "Clara wouldn't let me confront him about it. She said it would only make things worse for her mother."

"You said something about him taking her phone away. Why would he do that?" she asked.

"Yeah, I thought maybe he found out what she was doing and took it away as some kind of punishment," he admitted, and he seemed to think everyone knew what he was talking about.

"What was she doing that would upset him?" Leanne asked.

Christian looked from Leanne to Dalton like one of them had to know what he was about to say. "You didn't know?"

"I'm afraid not," Leanne said. Clara had another secret.

"She was searching for her father," he said, putting one hand on the table and grabbing his forehead with the other.

"Did she have any success?" This was the first Leanne had heard about her niece's search, and she wondered if her sister had uncovered it or was trying to cover it up. Sawmill would figure it out soon if he hadn't already based on her browsing history or cell phone records. Well, he'd deduce that she was looking for someone, even if he didn't know whom.

"Yeah." He ran his hand through his brown hair. "He lives in Dallas."

Dallas? A whole string of warning bombs detonated. Was that the real reason Clara had wanted to come live with her aunt? Why had her niece kept this from her?

There were so many secrets. First, Clara hid

just how bad things had gotten between her and her stepfather. She'd downplayed the fights between her mother and stepfather. And she'd hidden the fact that she was searching for her father.

Of course, trying to relate any of this emerging picture to the hanging and especially Dalton's friend nearly made her head explode with questions. Because the story developing was that Clara had located and contacted her father in Dallas, and either the man had decided for one reason or another to meet with her and get rid of her, or Gary had resented it and gotten rid of her. Tying the murder to a past crime in Cattle Barge could've been to confuse law enforcement.

Bethany didn't talk much about that part of her past. She hadn't said much more than she'd been in a dark place during dark times when she'd met Clara's father. She'd explained it like a bad storm and that, rather than focusing on the devastation, she wanted to rebuild her life. Just how bad had it been? How many more secrets were there under the layers?

Leanne shivered against the cold chill gripping her spine. Bethany didn't exactly have the best taste in men, but wouldn't she have known to stay away from someone so evil he could murder his own child when she reached out to him?

More questions swirled around in Leanne's head but she had trouble grabbing and holding on to just one. Had her sister been in a relationship with a murderer? Leanne had checked into Gary's background when the two had started dating and he'd been clean. She hadn't been around to do the same thing during Bethany's relationship to Clara's father.

"Did she tell you anything about her father?" Leanne hated to dredge this sore subject up with Bethany. Her sister had never wanted to discuss Clara's father and Leanne respected her privacy. Now, she wished she'd done more digging, demanded answers.

And yet, everything she knew about investigating murder said that the closest ring of people around the victim would most likely be as far as they had to look for the killer. Sadly, a woman's number one danger came from the person she lived with day to day, her spouse. Or in Clara's case, potentially her stepfather. Her own father killing her made no sense unless he had something to lose if news of her being his child came to light.

But what would it to do him?

And why would a stranger want to hurt his own daughter? All he would've had to do was blow her off and tell her to go away. She would've listened.

Unless there was more to the story and in Leanne's line of work, there almost always was.

What else were you hiding, Clara?

"CLARA'S FATHER WAS in a band, living in a loft with some friends and doing odd jobs. That's as far as we got during her search." The look in Christian's eyes was a sucker punch to Dalton's gut. Kids were honest about pain, unlike adults, who had years of practice burying theirs. Dalton should know. Seeing the kid in such a devastated state brought back a flood of memories for him, none of which he welcomed.

"Do you know his name?" Leanne asked.

"Adam Robinson, but he goes by Havoc because of his antics on stage," he supplied and it looked to be taking him a great effort not to break down. "His last name starts with an *h*. That's all I know."

Leanne had kicked into detective mode and Dalton wanted to protect Christian while still giving her the room she needed to dig for answers. The more questions she asked, the further the two cases moved away from each other. He could see that she was honing in on those closest to her niece for suspects and he couldn't argue the logic, no matter what that beating organ in the center of his chest wanted to say. Deep down, he wanted—needed!—these cases to be locked together in order to find answers for Alexandria's family and maybe put to rest some of his own torment.

This twist took him down a road he didn't want to go but couldn't ignore now that it was out there.

"Will you excuse us?" Dalton looked to Leanne for approval, still a little unsure why it suddenly seemed so important to get her stamp. This was shaky ground for him, because Dalton rarely cared what anyone other than his family thought about his actions.

Christian followed, swiping at a loose tear.

When they rounded the corner toward the side of the strip center, Dalton said, "I know what you're going through is hell, because I've been in your shoes."

The young man's eyes widened but he maintained focus on the patch of concrete in front of them. It was easy enough to see that the guy was doing everything he could not to break down. He needed to know it was okay to go with what he felt.

"I lost someone important to me when I was your age in a similar way," he said, leaving out the main difference of him being a prime suspect at the time. "Someone will be down to speak to you. Most likely a deputy. I want you to call me if he starts asking questions that make you scratch your head in any way."

Christian glanced up with a look of confusion.

"Trust me when I say these investigations can turn in all kinds of unexpected directions," he offered by way of explanation. "I want you to be prepared, so take this."

He pulled a card with his personal number and pressed it to the kid's palm. "Call me if any of the questioning seems out of line, like the deputy is grilling you or not taking you seriously. Definitely call me if he takes you in for questioning. Understand?"

"Sort of. I guess," Christian admitted.

"If you have a question about any of the news coverage coming out about her death, call me. I'll filter through it for you," he added. "Until then, it's best to stay away from news sites on the internet. There'll most likely be social media posts, too. You might want to avoid that if possible."

He knew all about how to avoid the media, including social sites. Then again, he'd never been on those to begin with. He'd left the state after his father was killed in order to get away from reporters for a little while. He came back the minute he heard Ella had been targeted, and thankfully, the man responsible was serving time.

"So, they don't know who did this to her?" he asked after a long pause and several tears.

"Not that I know of," he responded. "They called it a suicide at first, but we argued against it."

Dalton didn't need to finish that sentence because the kid was already shaking his head.

"She would never do that. We were happy. Everything was solid between us and we had a future." More tears streamed as the kid spoke.

"I know. They might not believe you. Stick to your story, which is the truth," Dalton said. "And here's the hard part. Find a way not to blame yourself."

"How am I supposed to do that? I never should've told her she should find her father. She was so unhappy and she said the situation with her aunt would be temporary, so when she said she wanted to look for her father I thought it was a good idea. I was trying to help. She was miserable with Gary and he was getting worse every—" He stopped midsentence. "Was he involved in this somehow?"

"We're not sure. On the surface, it looks like he could be," Dalton admitted. "But there was a similar case fourteen years ago that makes me think not."

And then it seemed to dawn on the kid.

"This happened to *your* girlfriend and you think it's the same guy," Christian said.

"The sheriff is going to come after you to ask questions, like where you were two days ago around midnight. Whether or not you and Clara were fighting. He might even throw in details in order to throw you off track," he said.

"That's easy—I was home watching my brother while my parents went out to dinner." He said it like it was a no-brainer, but a skilled investigator could pick it apart.

"How old is your brother?"

"He's twelve, but he doesn't like to stay home at night alone." Christian's eyebrow arched. "Why?"

"They'll ask, and you need to be prepared to answer just that honestly every time in case they try to play a head game with you," he said. Dalton needed to think of the right way to ask his next question. "Was Clara in any kind of trouble?"

"No. She was a good person."

"How about emotionally? She had a rough situation at home—"

"Oh, no. I can assure you she wouldn't try to hurt herself if that's where you're going with this," he said, and his tone was so matter-of-fact that Dalton wanted to believe him. One thing was certain, the kid believed it wholeheartedly.

"It was set up to look that way," Dalton admitted.

"She wouldn't hurt herself. We had a future. We were planning on going to college and then getting married our senior year before we start working." His words started breaking up as his emotions intensified with the memories of their plans. His face twisted in pure agony and Dalton's heart wrenched.

"I'm sorry, man. I know how much this hurts." Dalton put his hand on Christian's shoulder and was surprised when the kid barreled into him with a hug. Christian held on and seemed to let go of the pent-up emotions he'd been barely keeping at bay since hearing the news. Having a future ripped out from underneath like a rug unleashed more shock than Dalton had ever known at that age. He remembered feeling the exact same way Christian had at first. That initial shock followed by disbelief.

"She didn't deserve to have this happen," Christian said, sucking in another burst of air.

"No. She didn't. Neither did you," Dalton reassured. "I want you to use that number I gave you anytime you need to talk to me. Day or night. I'm here for you, buddy. I mean it. Any time."

"I will," Christian promised, and there was

honesty in his brown eyes. He wiped at his cheeks, swiping away tears while his head was down before asking, "We should probably go back to Clara's aunt."

"Not until I know you're all right," Dalton said.

Christian rocked his head, but there wasn't much conviction in his eyes. Dalton had just turned the kid's world on its axis and tossed it around as if in a hot dryer with no off button. Nothing would be the same after this day. Christian would look at the world differently from now on.

Dalton sure as hell did.

"How about you and your parents?" he asked.

"We're good. I mean, they care. They're not perfect, but they try," he admitted.

That was good to hear. Because he was going to need them and a whole lot more to get through the next couple of days, weeks. And especially when that angry beast called guilt that Dalton had contained for nearly a decade and a half started eating away at its chains.

Dalton led Christian around the corner and back to Leanne.

The sound of her ringtone broke the conversation. She quickly glanced at the screen and Dalton knew she was hoping for a call from the sheriff. He also doubted she'd get one.

"It's my babysitter," she announced along with an apology for needing to take the call.

"What happened?" Everything about her voice said she'd shifted into panic mode. Her back stiffened and she leaned into the earpiece, listening with the intensity of someone receiving the code to unlock a nuclear weapon.

"Where are you right now?" She listened for a response. "I'm on my way."

Leanne locked on to Dalton's gaze.

"A man wearing a ski mask just approached my daughter and her babysitter at the park." She flashed her eyes at him. "We have to go."

Chapter Twelve

"Your daughter will be picked up and brought to the ranch. I don't want you on the road. If someone's targeting her because of this investigation, they could be watching for you." Dalton made a few calls to set everything up.

Leanne seemed to be thinking up an argument. She'd told him the basic facts. Someone had approached the babysitter at the park and then made a play for Mila. Mrs. B, as Leanne called her, had pulled out her stun gun and blasted the guy with fifty thousand volts.

While he was flat on his back, squirming in pain, she got the baby safely inside her vehicle and called the police. Having a husband who'd spent most of his life in law enforcement and stressed the importance of being prepared helped her stay calm during the incident. Before Dallas Police could arrive, the man hopped to his feet and took off in the opposite direction. He'd managed to evade capture. Mrs. B had given as much of a description of the assailant as she could, considering the attacker was wearing a ski mask and it had all happened so fast.

He was roughly six feet tall, maybe a little shorter, and large.

Mrs. B and the baby were at the north central division. She was waiting for her husband and planned to stay with Mila until the flight crew and friend of the Butler family arrived. The crew was already in transit to pick up Mila and bring her safely to the ranch.

"It's the fastest way to get the two of you in the same location and keep both of you safe along the way," he continued. "I sent the best and she'll be in good hands."

After exhaling slowly, Leanne agreed.

He could only imagine what she must be feeling but based on her expression, it was as bad as he thought it might be.

"Christian, I'm sorry to leave you like this but we have to go," she said, her angst written across her expression.

"Don't worry about me," he said. Based on the change in his demeanor, he was more concerned for the little girl who might be in danger than his own emotions. Dalton had picked up right away that Christian was a good kid. His family didn't have enough money for college. Dalton had personal plans to see to it that a scholarship was set up to take care of tuition and anything else the kid needed. He deserved a future, and what had happened with his girlfriend would alter his thinking for the rest of his life. Dalton would talk to Ed Staples, the family lawyer, about the scholarship and maybe setting Christian up with a counselor and money in a trust to take care of college-related expenses. Dalton had no idea how to make any of this right, but based on his own personal experience of going inside himself, he knew *not* talking about it with someone was a worse idea. And yet, that's exactly what he'd done. "A friend of mine is going to call you in a day or two. His name is Ed Staples and he's a lawyer."

Christian's eyes grew wide again.

"Not because I think you're going to need him to get yourself out of trouble, but because he's going to check on a few things for me and then contact you. Okay?" Dalton asked.

"Thank you," Christian said before the two embraced in a man-hug. "Talking to you about it is helping a lot."

This kid had no idea just how long the road ahead of him was going to be, but Dalton had a good feeling about Christian and he'd do whatever it took to help shorten the journey to healing.

"Anyone at home right now?" Dalton asked.

"My mom is," he responded and it was obvious from his expression that he was still in shock.

"A car will be here in a few minutes to pick you up." Dalton pushed a few buttons on his phone to order a service. "The driver will take you home to be with her."

"I have work to—"

"I'll make sure you have a job when you return," Leanne said.

"I need this in order to go to college—"

"Consider me a family friend who wants to help and can," Dalton said. "Don't worry about money."

He could see the hesitation in Christian's eyes. The kid, his family, had learned to get by using hard work and not handouts.

"This isn't charity. I'm investing in you because I believe in you. And we'll figure out a way for you to pay it back some day. Deal?" Dalton extended his hand.

Christian seemed tentative at first, but then he gripped Dalton's hand and gave it a good shake.

"I don't know how to thank you," he said, and there was so much gratitude in his eyes.

"You will," was all Dalton said before entering the kid's number into his phone. The two finished saying their goodbyes while Leanne disappeared to speak to his supervisor. With the right support, Dalton felt that Christian would be okay. And he intended to check up on the kid. "Call your mother and let her know that you're on your way home."

Helping made Dalton feel another peak of light in his soul. Something he'd stuffed away long ago surfaced and a little of his darkness released.

Leanne returned and he ushered her into the SUV. They were pulling out of the parking lot as the driver was pulling in.

"He's a good kid," Dalton said as he navigated onto the highway. It felt good to be able to help someone else. Dalton had never been comfortable with the money he'd been born into. He'd never needed much to be comfortable. But being able to help someone else who needed it felt right in a way he'd never experienced. He'd put it to Ella's influence. His older sister was always out doing good somewhere in the community. But this desire to release some of the grip on his old ghosts and be a better man came from somewhere else.

And it probably had a lot to do with the person sitting next to him. He wanted to be her comfort. "You can take my phone if it'll make you feel better. I asked for updates about your daughter's location every fifteen minutes."

"I'd like that very much," Leanne said without hesitation. She picked up the phone sitting in between them and studied the screen.

"If you pull up the map feature you'll be able to track your daughter in real time."

"Seriously?" The sense of hope and relief spoken in that one word was all the thanks he needed. "This is beyond." She looked up from the screen for a second. "Thank you. It's hard to focus on anything else for long after what happened."

"It's understandable." And probably what made her a good mother. Though, he'd keep that last part to himself.

The crew was half an hour from the ranch as Dalton pulled past the security gate at Hereford and then parked the SUV in his usual spot.

"Does anyone know where Gary is?" Dalton asked as he pulled the key from the ignition.

"No. But I'm half-surprised he isn't here throwing a fit on your front lawn," Leanne said with an eye roll.

"He'd never get past security," Dalton quipped. The past few days had been heavy—for good reason—and he wanted to put a smile on her face, even if it didn't last.

Glancing over at her, Dalton couldn't help but notice the exhaustion lines on her face.

"You think it was him?" She checked her watch. Depending on when he'd been released, he might've had time to make the drive. Although, when he really thought about it the timing was off.

"It's possible. Then there's Havoc to consider."

"We need a description of him," Leanne said. "But we don't have a last name."

"How many men named Havoc can there be in Dallas who are also in a band?" he asked.

"Of course. I'm not thinking straight or…"

"Your thoughts are right where they're supposed to be. On making sure your daughter is safe," he said.

She pulled out her phone and after a couple of minutes said, "According to Blue Potato Bar in Deep Ellum, his band is scheduled to play next month." She paused long enough to pull up a picture of the band. "These guys are skinny. It's hard to believe any one of them would have the strength to carry her. Also, according to his website he played a gig on December 7 in Oklahoma. There'd be witnesses."

"Then we just ruled someone out."

Silence stretched on for a few minutes after Leanne put her phone away.

"You did a good thing for Christian," she said. "Thank you."

Those two words cracked a little more of the casing inside his chest. Allowing a little more light to bleed through. "He's a decent kid. Sure as hell didn't deserve any of this."

"Neither did you," she said quietly.

"I wasn't as good as him," Dalton said in response.

"You couldn't be this good of a man if you weren't a decent kid. I have enough experience dealing with people from all walks of life to be certain of that," she said. "Kids make mistakes, Dalton. It's part of growing up."

He let the words sit between them.

"I didn't ask on the way over because part of me didn't want to know. But before I go in there, is my sister here?"

"SHE STAYED," HE said and hope lit in Leanne's chest like a fledgling campfire in a severe storm watch.

So many emotions bubbled to the surface that Leanne was at a loss to contain them. Rather than deal with any of those, she distracted herself by leaning over and kissing him.

The second her lips pressed to his she realized her mistake. It was most likely the primal need for proof of life that had her melting into the kiss, hungry and wanting more.

He brought his hand up to the back of her neck and cradled it as he drove his tongue inside her mouth. There was no hesitation in his skilled movements and his actions robbed her of her breath.

An explosion of need rocketed through her. Need to be with this strong man. Need to feel his arms around her. Need to...*escape*. Hold on a minute.

The last thought caused her to put on the brakes. She cursed her overactive mind as she pulled away. The best kiss she'd had in...her... What?... Entire life? And she couldn't shut down random thoughts that had run wild. The realization about the kiss was sad but accurate. It was the best she'd ever had. Not even with Mila's father had Leanne felt that kind of sizzle.

"I'm sorry," she said, turning and reaching for the door.

He stopped her with a hand on her shoulder and the shock of electricity stemming from contact reminded her why the two of them together was a bad idea. There was too much stray voltage that could damage everything around them.

Besides, all she could think about was seeing her daughter again, holding her and making sure the little girl was safe.

"Don't be." And then he removed his hand—leaving an immediate feeling of cold in its place—before getting out of the SUV.

"How do most murder investigations work?" Dalton asked.

"What do you mean?"

"Who do you usually start investigating first?" He stopped next to his vehicle.

"Those closest to the victim. Family. Friends." She arched a brow. "Why?"

"Because we've done that. We talked to your sister, Clara's boyfriend and her stepdad. What happens if all the family members check out?" He leaned an elbow against his SUV.

"We funnel out from there." Leanne took in a deep breath. "We'd look at friends, known associations, places the victim frequented."

"I keep going back to the tracks leading up to the tree. There was only one set, which means there was no resistance. If they were drugged, who has access?" His eyes sparked with possibilities.

"A pharmacist comes to mind first. Dentist or doctor." She studied his face.

"The town pharmacist has a son who could be the right age. What about a bus driver? Someone they knew or had met."

She rocked her head in agreement. "Not to put a damper on your ideas but both girls were upset and maybe a little naive. They were at a vulnerable age. A stranger could disarm them and lower their guard if he knew what he was doing."

"Let's think about on it some more," he said.

She followed suit and with every step toward the main house, her tension increased. By the time she walked across the threshold and marched into the kitchen, her pulse blazed. Her sister sat at the table where Leanne had last seen Hampton. She was smiling and playing with her son.

When Bethany looked up, there was an empty expression in her eyes. Was it possible she didn't know Gary had been released? Anger shot through Leanne at thinking he might be involved in her daughter's attempted abduction. Why would he do that?

The answer came almost immediately. To punish her.

"How's everything going in here?" Leanne asked, suddenly afraid to bring up the subject. Maybe she could work on her sister a little bit and convince her to stick around and get healthy.

"Good," Bethany said.

Hampton looked up with a huge smile plastered on his face. "Lee-Lee."

"Hello, buddy." It was good to see him genuinely happy. Her heart squeezed, thinking how much she missed Mila. Her little girl was safe. She was on her way.

Leanne refocused on Hampton. She'd worried that taking him out of his environment would be stressful. Turns out, he was acting like he was on the best vacation ever. She could admit the ranch held a certain unexplainable magic that had her tension ratcheting down a few notches.

"He's out," Bethany said with those same dead eyes.

"I know." Leanne was surprised by her sister's reaction.

Tears welled and Bethany turned her head as though she didn't want her son to see her cry.

"Can I play?" Dalton seemed to pick up on the tension. He pulled out a chair on the other side of Hampton. "I used to hide this truck so my brother wouldn't get to play with it."

"You did?" Hampton giggled like the two were conspiring.

Leanne moved to Bethany's other side and took a seat. "I'm sorry I didn't call. I wanted to tell you in person."

"How do you know?" There was such hollowness to her voice that it made Leanne's heart ache. She wished she could take her sister's pain away.

Leanne held up her cell.

"He said if I didn't come home now that I shouldn't bother. There wouldn't be one to come back to," Bethany said quietly. She glanced toward Hampton who was invested in playing with Dalton.

"It's an idle threat. You know that, right?" By

no means did Leanne want her sister to go back to that creep, and she had yet to determine if he was also a criminal. Bethany needed to make a decision. Trying to force her would only push her toward him instead of away. Leanne also knew the pitfall of tying up her self-worth with a man who didn't deserve it.

The first real relationship Leanne had been in after graduating high school had been with an older man who'd manipulated her into thinking she was special to him. He'd said all the right things—things she'd wanted to hear but didn't have the experience to know whether or not they were sincere—and she'd taken the bait. Then the little insults had started.

He'd commented about her hairstyle not fitting her face and that he thought she'd enjoy it more if she cut it short. When she accepted that criticism, because she'd always been good at seeing her flaws, he added a few more. Her clothes were too tight. Her lipstick too bright. Later, she'd realized that he'd believed in breaking her down and by making her believe she was less than him so she would stay. It didn't take long to see through him, but she'd allowed herself to fall for the guy—or at least that's what she'd believed at eighteen—and he'd been a first-rate jerk. She'd picked up what was left of her self-esteem and moved on.

The only good thing about youthful relationships was that while emotions might run high, they didn't run as deep.

Walking away from him had proven the easy part. Trying to regain confidence in herself and her judgment about people had been the tricky stuff. Leanne had always been too hard on herself.

Bethany seemed to be teetering on an emotional ledge. Leanne needed to know which way she was going to fall, because one of those choices would kill her ability to help her sister. In these situations, a straightforward approach was always best.

"Are you going back to him?" Leanne asked outright.

Bethany drew a sharp breath and the attention of Hampton, who locked on to her.

"Mommy?"

"It's okay, sweetie. Mommy's fine," she reassured.

When Hampton went back to playing with the toys, she leaned toward Leanne and said, "How am I supposed to tell my little boy his sister is gone?"

"It'll be hard but he needs to know." Leanne realized that her sister had changed the subject.

"He wasn't at the hunting lodge the other night.

I called my friend and she said they didn't go. He went drinking instead," Bethany admitted.

Which was suspect but didn't necessarily mean that Gary was a murderer or kidnapper.

"He and Clara didn't get along too good and especially lately. Those two were oil and water," she said.

Leanne further wanted to point out that they were like gasoline and fire, but she let her sister continue.

"What if he was invo—" Bethany released a sob and surprised Leanne by wrapping her arms around her. Bethany's body trembled.

"Then we'll nail the bastard," Leanne said low and into her sister's ear. "But right now you need to let Hampton know what's going on."

A look of resignation passed behind Bethany's eyes. She walked over to her son and dropped down to his level. She said a few quiet words to him as she patted him on the back and both cried.

"GARY'S ALIBI IS blown and it's only a matter of time before the sheriff finds out," Leanne said to Dalton.

The two had walked outside for fresh air after Bethany had calmed down and decided to take a nap with Hampton.

"She told you that?" he asked, wide-eyed, and

she fully understood his surprise at the admission. Bethany had been so adamant about protecting him. The woman was on an emotional roller coaster as her world crumbled around her. Without Mila there, Leanne could relate to the out-of-control feeling.

"Yes."

"Did you advise her to tell Sawmill?" His dark brow arched in clear surprise that she might not have after looking at her.

"Of course." But something had been nagging her from the start. They'd been focused on Gary. Too focused. While he might explain Clara's murder, it didn't make sense that he would've known Alexandria. She needed to look at this from another perspective. "Can I see those pictures again?"

He pulled out his cell and thumbed the photo application open. "Which ones?"

"The tree." She moved next to him and her arm grazed his, causing a little too much electricity to jolt through her.

He handed the phone to her to let her scroll through the photos until she stopped on one of the tree and examined it closer.

"How high is this branch?" she asked, knowing she was heading into dark territory with him because it was the one the girls had been hung from. It hit her, too, in a spot dark and deep.

Maybe shared pain was the reason she felt so connected to a man she barely knew. Although, after spending two intense days with him, she felt like she'd known him her entire life.

Looking at the photo again made every beat of her heart hurt. Her brain scrambled from the onslaught of emotion bearing down. But she was on a mission, so she shoved those thoughts, those emotions to the side. She'd deal with them later, and she'd pay the price for bottling them up.

"About seven feet tall," he said, looking closer.

"The rope probably hung a foot and a half from the branch to the victim's neck." She wouldn't use the victims' names anymore. She couldn't. It would be too personal, and she had to keep a laser focus. "How tall was your friend?"

"She was around five feet five inches," he supplied. "Why?"

"You said something about the knot that has been sticking with me," she admitted. "He's proving a point. With one pull in the right direction, the girls could've freed themselves."

"Thinking about it takes me down a different path than Gary. I'm guessing it does the same for you." He rubbed the two-day scruff on his chin, as he seemed to be catching on. Dark circles cradled his intense blue eyes.

"If my calculations are right, the victims' feet would've been inches from the ground," she added. "Meaning he might've been proving a point."

"Or shoving it in our faces," he added bitterly.

"And what is he ultimately saying?"

"That he's smarter than everyone else," he deduced.

"This guy thinks he's better than us. Superior," she said, and her shoulders deflated. "Gary doesn't fit that profile, and I know for a fact he was never a Boy Scout."

"I know."

"This person knows the area well, which leads me to believe he's local and not someone passing through," she added. "I don't think Gary's ever been to Cattle Barge before."

"Except that he was the one who chose this place to live, right?"

"True. I thought about that, too. He came here for work but then lost another job," she said.

"Wouldn't that shoot him up the suspect list? He's frustrated. Wants to show the world his real power. That he's better than everyone else," he theorized.

"The arguments with my sister intensified as a result of him losing his job. And I think that might've been his outlet." She paced in front of the house. "I keep going back to the fact that he's a hothead. The timing of the killings might've been opportunistic but I believe the acts were premeditated."

Dalton muttered a curse and something about the man responsible being right under his nose this whole time. "Why would he wait fourteen years to strike again?"

"My best guess is that he's a serial killer. It's not uncommon for them to have long cooling-off periods in between killings," she confided. "Was anything missing from the victim in your case? Jewelry? Article of clothing?"

"I remember the sheriff asking where her other earring was. It struck me as odd at the time." Dalton raked his hand through his hair as though trying to tame the out-of-control curls. The fact that his thoughts were heavy was written all over the tension in his face and body.

"He most likely kept it as a souvenir," she said with disdain, and wondered what he'd kept of Clara's and if the sheriff would even tell her if anything was missing. That familiar anger raged inside her and she knew it would cloud her judgment if she didn't keep it in check. She couldn't afford anything less than crystal clear focus.

What if she gave Bethany a list of questions

to ask? Surely, the sheriff wouldn't deny information from a mother who was curious about the investigation into her daughter's death. Sawmill had seen her and Bethany react to each other. He wouldn't assume the two were talking. This could work.

"I'm guessing by the spark in your eye that you're thinking the same thing I am," Dalton said. "Do you think Bethany's up to asking the sheriff a few questions?"

Chapter Thirteen

"My sister wants to find out what happened to Clara. I can't deny that it might be so she can find out if Gary's in the clear or cheating on her. If he's not involved, she might actually take him back," Leanne said with disgust.

"Hampton's a good kid," Dalton said. "He deserves a better life than watching his father berate his mother."

"My sister needs to tell him about Clara." A tear rolled down her cheek. "My family must seem crazy to someone like you," she said.

"Families are complicated and none of them are perfect," he responded quickly and it made her wonder about his. She already knew he was close to his siblings, but he hadn't said much about his parents. "Were your mother and father close?"

"I'm not sure. My mom took off when we were little. My father was Maverick Mike Butler. He didn't exactly light a campfire every Friday night, rally the children and talk about his feelings." There was no emotion in his voice.

"So you don't know much about their story?" She wanted to know more about the handsome cowboy. More than she could read in a headline. And a part of her couldn't deny that she wanted him to confide in her.

"Everything my father did made news. And yet, he managed to keep many of his personal exploits out of the public eye. Can't say there was much between us other than him giving me and Dade orders," he said.

"So the two of you weren't close?" she asked.

"My brother and me, hell, yes. But Maverick Mike was a different story," he admitted.

"Do you miss him?" She glanced around at all the holiday decorations. Christmas was the loneliest time of year for her since her mother died. She'd been looking forward to this year's, as it would be Mila's first. Clara would have been with them and the three of them together would have been the most family she'd had under one roof in as long as she could remember.

But then the desperate call from Clara had come.

"His presence? Yeah. The man? Not as much as I probably should." His admission caught her off guard. He was opening up and telling her something very real about himself.

"I'm sorry," she said softly for lack of anything better. She said it all the time in her work and meant it, but it had never felt so hollow until now. Was it because she suddenly realized how inadequate those words were after losing Clara? Her niece didn't even have a name anymore. She would forever be referred to as a victim.

A tear surprised her, springing from her eye and spilling onto her cheek. She mumbled another apology, but Dalton responded by lifting her chin until her eyes came up to meet his. His complicated family relationship made him more relatable to her and the pull toward him even more intense.

"Don't apologize for showing emotion." He thumbed the tear from her cheek and there was so much tenderness in that one move.

"If it makes you feel any better, this is Mila's first Christmas and I don't even have one decoration up. No tree. Nothing. Looks like I won't be up for mother of the year."

"That doesn't make you a bad mother."

She flashed her eyes at him.

Leanne couldn't think of one word to say against the tug she felt. She wanted to argue that her timing was awful—and it was—but she couldn't deny the urge to kiss Dalton again.

So, she popped onto her tiptoes and did just that.

He groaned as she pressed her lips to his and then his tongue slicked across hers. This time, he wrapped his arms around her waist and pulled her flush against his hard, muscled wall of a chest.

She brought her hands up to brace herself, but instead found herself gripping his shoulders and digging her nails into him, pulling him closer. Desire rocketed through her and sensual shivers skittered across her exposed skin.

His mouth covered hers and both of their breathing intensified. Electricity hummed though her nerve endings, awakening every cell and she surrendered to the feelings engulfing her like wildfire in a dry forest.

The bucket of cold water came in the form of tires on gravel out front. *Mila?*

DALTON PULLED BACK, muttered a curse along with his frustration about timing before threading his fingers with Leanne's. He led her toward a shortcut to get to the small parking lot.

Dalton had seen the serious side of Leanne. He'd seen the devastated side. But nothing prepared him for seeing her tender side. The look on her face when she saw her daughter had the effect of showering light into a black hole. Everything about Leanne relaxed when she looked at her little girl.

The way her daughter's face lit up when she saw her mother was enough to melt a diamond in the icebox. The little girl was all round angelic face and big brown eyes, the color of honey just like her mother's. She had a sprinkling of hair, her fist in her mouth and a bright smile.

His heart stirred and cracks in the veneer exploded at seeing the interaction between mother and daughter.

He needed to get his thoughts together, because he was thinking about the three of them as a family.

Dalton excused himself and walked away.

After refilling his coffee cup, he stepped onto the back porch in order to breathe in the fresh air and think about what they'd discussed.

Taking a seat and leaning forward, he thought about the kind of person who would have access to the girls. Someone they'd be comfortable with. Years ago, he'd read in a crime journal that predators usually knew their targets and gained their trust beforehand. That could explain why neither girl showed signs of a struggle. Was there some type of drug involved? Leanne had made a good point about the girls being vulnerable. He couldn't speak for Clara but Alexandria had been angry. She might've acted out of character or put herself in a bad situation.

The local pharmacist, Larry Wentworth, had been living in the community for three generations. Dalton went to school with his son, Bartholomew. It would take someone strong to lift the girls and Mr. Wentworth had to be in his early sixties. Everything about him was short. Short height. Short legs. Short hands. Due to the fact that he was both short and thin, Dalton doubted he was strong enough to lift the girls, let alone pull off the murders.

Bartholomew was Dalton's age and he could be strong enough. Had he married? Dalton thought about the fact that many of his classmates had settled down by now. Even Dade had found love in a stable relationship.

He and Cadence, the baby of the family, were the only two who were still single.

Personally, Dalton was nowhere near ready for that kind of commitment. Not until he brought justice to Alexandria's murderer. Not until he got past the anger he felt toward the Mav. And not until he could feel something in his chest besides anger and betrayal. His mother had disappeared when he was too young to remember her. Alexandria had been taken from him. And the only woman he'd been serious enough about to consider moving in with had walked out days before signing the lease, saying that he was still in love with a ghost.

Was that true?

Dalton refocused on the coffee mug, rolling it around in his hands. Alexandria deserved justice.

What was he missing?

There was no way Christian had done anything to hurt Clara. It was obvious the kid was head-over-heels in love with her. He was a decent kid, hardworking, with good grades and a solid future. He seemed to have the support of his family. He didn't fit the stereotype of a murderer, not to mention the fact that the two were on solid ground, according to Christian. He had no reason to hurt her and he would've been three years old at the time of Alexandria's murder.

Dalton knew that losing her in this way would affect every relationship Christian had with the opposite sex for the rest of his life. It had for him.

"Can I join you?" Bethany asked from the door, surprising him.

"Be my guest." Dalton gestured toward the chair opposite him, the one Leanne had sat in earlier that morning.

"Thank you."

The screen door opened behind him.

"Got anything to drink out here?" Bethany took the seat and pulled her legs up, wrapping her arms around them.

"Afraid not." And she didn't need anything, especially with the emotional state she'd been in.

"I can't imagine what you must think of our family," she said sheepishly. "We must seem crazy to someone who grew up in such a nice place."

"All families have their moments," he said. "Believe me, ours is just like everyone else's."

"I doubt it," she said, waving a hand around.

"Right. The money. Don't get me wrong, we're grateful to have food on the table and a roof over our heads. Kids need more than that," he defended.

There was an awkward silence.

"I keep running through everything in my head, and I just can't imagine Gary doing something like this. He and Clara had their differences, but…" She twisted her fingers together.

Dalton didn't speak. This wasn't the time to play his hand, and she might confess something that could lead them to the killer.

Bethany rubbed her eyes.

She released a sob. "It's possible. I can't deny it. He wasn't where he said he'd be the other night."

"I know I said it before but I couldn't be sorrier for your loss," he said.

"She was a good girl," she admitted. "Never got into trouble at school. Well, except when other kids bullied her, and then she'd get called out for talking when she told them to leave her alone. Seems like the teachers here have their favorites, and those kids get away with…" She stopped herself from finishing the sentence as she rubbed her eyes again.

"This town can be pretty tight. Folks have grown up together and it can be hard to break in," he said.

"My Clara was smart and a few kids didn't seem to like the fact that she made better grades," she continued.

"What about that bullying you mentioned? Did any of them make any real threats to her safety?" he asked.

Bethany shrugged tired shoulders. "She may have mentioned a couple of names of kids who elbowed her into her locker. You know, typical acting up."

"Did she tell the principal or talk to a teacher?" From the sounds of it, she was enduring more than standard jokes. It seemed like there were even more ways to make kids miserable these days. Forget the grapevine that ended with a handful of smart-mouthed kids. Now, rumors could be spread via the internet on social media.

"Said it would only make things worse," she said.

"Than what?" he scoffed. And then he really thought about it. High school for someone who didn't feel like they fit in could be hard. Scratch that. It could be hell. Especially if that person was being bullied. Being in a new environment was never easy.

He didn't want to believe it was possible that local kids could've been hazing her and not just because that would mean his theory that the cases were linked would go up in smoke. Part of him, and it was a very big part, wanted to believe that kids in Cattle Barge were decent human beings. But he didn't want to be selfish when a young woman had lost her life. He had to consider the possibility that Clara's situation had nothing to do with Alexandria's murder and that even in a small community kids could go unchecked.

Kids were smart and they could dig up facts on the internet no one else seemed able to. He wouldn't take anything for granted. As much as he wanted—no, needed—to put Alexandria's case to rest, he had to make sure the right person was caught and prosecuted.

Was it possible that a few kids could've found

out the details of Alexandria's case? Could Clara's "suicide" have been staged to look like she'd done it to herself? He'd read some horrific stories about the cruelty of college kids' hazing pledges to fraternities. Dalton had never been the "join-in" type, and he couldn't see why anyone would want to be part of a club so badly that they'd be willing to chuck their dignity.

Guess his independent streak would've never allowed him to be that desperate to conform. From what he'd been told about Clara so far, neither was she and he respected her for it. Such a shame that a life could be cut down so young.

Thinking about his conversation with Bethany caused something to click. He and Leanne might not be able to get to her laptop, but they could check out her profile and recent posts. Maybe there'd be a clue in there, because he was getting frustrated by the lack of anything else to go on.

And he wondered how reliable any information from Bethany would be.

"How often have you been taking the medication lately?" Dalton asked.

"Not much. I just take it when I need it," she said a little too defensively. Dalton knew on instinct that she was downplaying her usage.

And that could mean she'd missed a lot of signs. At this point, they'd covered Gary well enough. The sheriff was investigating him and Dalton had to believe if there was anything there, Sawmill would see it.

"What about her father? Have you heard from him?" he asked.

Bethany seemed taken aback by the questions.

"He hasn't been around since Clara was a baby," she scoffed.

Opening up to her about his personal life might build a sense of comradery, which in turn could help her relax and open up a bit more. She'd been on the defensive with her sister in every conversation he'd observed so far.

"Same with my mother," he admitted.

Bethany's eyes widened with shock. "I'm sorry for saying this, but I figured someone who grew up in a place like this would have a perfect life."

"Most people think the same thing."

"I guess that saying about money not being able to buy happiness is true," she said before adding, "It's sure hard to be happy without it, though."

"Money isn't the source of happiness or the root of evil," he said. "A man only needs enough to put a decent roof over his family and good food on the table. Whatever else he does with it is up to him."

Using it to help a decent family in need of a break sure as hell made him feel proud, though. Maybe that was the trick to having money and feeling good about it, sharing it with people who deserved better than what they'd been handed.

"You don't think her father knows anything about what happened, do you?" he asked, trying to gauge if she knew about her daughter reaching out. Based on what he knew about their relationship, he didn't think Clara would have mentioned it to her mother, but there were a lot of spying devices that could be used to monitor texts, social media pages and emails. Most devices or applications were easy enough to find on the internet following a quick search. Privacy wasn't guaranteed when it came to using technology, no matter how much people felt secure with it.

"No. He had no interest in her," she supplied.

"Even so, he deserves to know what happened to his daughter." It wasn't Dalton's place to tell Bethany that Clara had reached out to her biological father. He and Leanne needed to make an appointment with the sheriff to discuss it, along with a couple of other theories, in order to cover all bases.

If Sawmill locked on to an idea, he might have a tough time seeing alternatives. If they could shed light on an area that he hadn't considered and help with the investigation of Clara's murder, he might just find out what had happened to Alexandria, too.

And then something must've dawned on Bethany, because she squinted her eyes and her lips compressed.

"I didn't think much about it at the time, but she mentioned some guy hanging around and giving her the creeps," she said.

"Recently?" he asked.

"She brought it up not long after school started again. I guess that's why I didn't think about it the other day," she supplied. "I should've listened to her more."

"But she didn't say anything lately?"

"No. But that could be my fault." The familiar pains of guilt darkened her features. "When school started, she got real homesick. Seems like San Antonio was all she could talk about. When she wasn't singing its praises, she was complaining about everything in Cattle Barge. I didn't think she was giving it a chance here, so I got on her case pretty hard. I guess I reached a boiling point, you know?" She looked to him for what he interpreted as approval, or maybe just a sign he wasn't judging her too harshly. Based on her expression and the pain wilting her body, he figured she was doing enough of that on her own.

"Teenagers can make everything overblown and seem worse than it is," he said. "You wanted her to give it a chance here."

She nodded and seemed grateful for the understanding.

He remembered enough of his and Dade's teenage years to know his statement was true, even before Alexandria's murder.

A thought struck. Was he remembering all the harsh words and actions of his father while excluding anything good the man had done? It was so easy, especially for a young person, to file someone in the "good" or "bad" category, leaving them there whether they still deserved it or not.

Dalton could admit that his father had turned a new leaf in recent years. In holding on to his hurt from the past, he'd robbed himself of getting to know the man his father had become.

"She describe the guy to you?" he asked.

"No. But I'm not at all surprised with the way I shut her down. She didn't mention him again or the bullying, but I could see how unhappy she was." A sob escaped. "I should've let her live with one of her friends in San Antonio and then my baby would still be alive."

"Hindsight might give us perfect vision, but I can see how much you love Clara," he defended, knowing she would carry that guilt for the rest of her life. "You didn't know this would happen, and you can't blame yourself."

Didn't saying that make him feel like the world's biggest hypocrite? Hadn't he been carrying around guilt over Alexandria's death for the past fourteen years? It had become part of him, squeezing the light out of everything inside him.

Leanne was breaking down his walls, though. He had no idea what that meant for the future but he wanted to be around her, in her life somehow.

But could he?

Was there even room?

Chapter Fourteen

Bethany and Hampton were resting. Mila was down for her afternoon nap. Hampton had insisted the baby be allowed to stay in his room and Leanne figured he was most likely missing Clara, so she agreed.

Walking helped Leanne think when she was stuck and this case had her head spinning.

Stepping out the back door, she saw Dalton walk into the barn carrying a bag of something. Feed? She followed him, wanting to pick his brain again. He'd been quiet after leaving her alone with Mila.

"Hello?" she said as she stepped inside the partially opened door.

"In here," he responded, and she could tell that he was in one of the horse stalls.

"I figured a barn on a ranch like this would be booming," she said.

"Not at this time of day. Everyone's out taking care of the cattle, checking fences and making necessary repairs."

"This one's beautiful." She walked over to the mare.

"This old gray mare?" he asked with a smile, and she could see how much pride he had in the horse. "Name's Lizzie. She's mine. Rescued her from Lone Star Park after a trainer took pity on her when she lost a race and then found out she had health problems."

"What did her owner say?" she balked.

"He wanted her euthanized. Billy 'Big Heart' Willy slipped her out the back door, looking for someone, anyone, who promised not to race her again. He'd lose his job if his boss saw her on the track again." He patted her on her long neck. "She's been with me six years with no signs of slowing down."

Lizzie looked like she was actually smiling.

"I feel like I should know more about horses growing up in Texas. There aren't a lot of barns where I grew up in east Dallas," she confessed. "I know you were born into ranching, but is it what you wanted to do?"

"Yes. There's something about being on the land, working with my hands that makes me feel alive. I've always known my place was at Hereford," he admitted. "What about you? Did you always want to be a cop?"

"Me? No. Not until I was a teenager and lost my mother. I started getting serious about my future then. We shared a small apartment and whenever we were home at the same time, which was rare, we were climbing on top of each other." She smiled at the fond memory. "I decided that I wanted a career with a solid future."

"I guess we both lost people we loved early in life."

Was that part of the pull she felt toward the handsome cowboy?

"The two of you were close," he acknowledged.

"We were more like sisters, because she was a young mother and we were figuring it all out together," she said. "Times were hard but we made it through."

In losing her mother, she realized that she'd lost her belief in people being good. Letting anyone truly get close to her afterward had been off the table.

She stood there, looking into his eyes and she could feel the change in temperature. Her thighs heated as they locked gazes. Her pulse pounded. And rational thought blew out the window.

He stood there like he was debating his next move.

Which lasted for all of about a minute until he

stalked toward her, brought his hands to cradle her neck and then kissed her.

She could taste coffee on his lips as he deepened the kiss.

This time, any resistance faded, her mind quieted and her body ached with need as he pulled her flush against his solid wall of a chest. Her breasts swelled and her nipples beaded as his hands slid underneath her blouse and cupped her lacy bra.

Heat engulfed them as urgency roared, building with a tempo she'd never experienced before.

She pulled back enough to say, "Don't stop this time, Dalton."

It was all the encouragement he seemed to need, as she pressed her fingertips into his shoulders. Tilting her head toward his gave him better access to her mouth and his tongue lunged inside.

He made a guttural groaning noise from low in his throat, and it was the sexiest sound she'd ever heard.

She dropped her hands and started unbuttoning her blouse. Her body had so much pent-up need that her fingers trembled. Dalton joined her and helped her out of her shoulder holster and shirt before walking her to an office across the hall.

The room was the size of two horse pens. Concrete flooring was covered with a soft rug. Furnishings were simple. Across from a hand-made desk and chair stood a comfortable-looking leather love seat.

Leanne placed her shoulder holster with her weapon on top of the desk along with her shirt. She kicked her mules off before unsnapping her bra and shrugging out of it. Next, she shimmed out of the borrowed jeans, taking her lacy underwear off in the same motion.

When she looked up at Dalton again, he was completely naked and her pulse skyrocketed at the sight of him. Anticipation mounted as he stood there, looking at her, appreciating her. It had been a very long time since she'd felt adored by a man, maybe never. Certainly not with this level of intensity.

"You're beautiful," he said. Her stomach free-fell in the best possible way.

She was normally embarrassed by her body and especially now that she'd had a baby. Her hips were fuller than before and there were marks that had never disappeared.

The hot cowboy didn't seem to notice any of her flaws.

"So are you," she said with a flirty smile. Her gaze slid over his chest and down to that dark patch of hair. A little farther south and she could see how much he liked seeing her naked based on his straining erection.

It turned her on.

"I want to feel your hands on me, Dalton," she said.

It took only three strides for him to stand in front of her. He pulled a condom from the wallet on the desk and she helped him put it on, stretching it over his tip and down his stiff length.

And then he tilted her head back and captured her mouth. Her bones went liquid when he kissed her so thoroughly, her body hummed with anticipation as she stood there.

Every cell inside her cried out to touch him, so she did. She smoothed her flat palm across his muscled chest, letting her fingers glide over the strong lines. The thought of making love to someone had never seemed this good of an idea or *this* right.

It should scare her.

But it didn't.

DALTON'S HEART THUNDERED as he explored Leanne's taste. He feathered kisses along her jawline, her neck before cupping her full breast with one hand and slicking his tongue across the other. Her back arched and her nipples beaded, flooding him with heat.

He picked her up and repositioned her on the edge of his desk before sliding his tongue south. He gripped her sweet round bottom as he slicked his tongue inside her sweet heat. She moaned and wiggled her hips as he moved his mouth along the inside of her thigh until she begged for release.

He stood and she wrapped her legs around his midsection before grinding against his erection.

When she scooted closer until his tip entered her mound, he had to strain to maintain control—which threw him for a loop. He'd never been early to the races, but she was so damn sexy with her curves and silky skin that he nearly detonated before it got interesting.

Her bare breasts pressed against his chest as she pulled closer, digging her fingers into his shoulders as he entered her.

"Dalton." She said his name so low, but it was the sweetest sound. He wanted to hear it again and again until she screamed it in release, so he dipped inside a little deeper, waiting to make sure she was okay.

Her wet heat surrounding his erection was the second time he almost lost it. *Damn, Butler. Way to slow down.*

She was that sexy. Her body was one thing and, yes, it was his idea of perfection. But the sexy sparkle in her honey-browns when she looked at him threw him into a whole new strato-sphere of attraction. She was sharp and warm, a rare combination of spunk and tenderness.

And when she bucked him in deeper, he gripped her sweet bottom and drove them both home.

The next few minutes were a frenzy of tongues melding, hands exploring and friction building.

Deeper, she welcomed him, answering his strides with a fever pitch until her muscles strung tight and he could sense she was on the edge.

Thrusting. Faster. Harder.

She cried out his name in sweet ecstasy as her muscles contracted around his hard length.

His pace was steady as he guided her toward that sweet release she craved until she shattered around him.

And then he detonated, too. Driving steady and deep until everything drained from him.

Panting, he held on to her. Both seemed to need this moment in the present. Because experience had taught them tomorrow wasn't guaranteed. Both seemed to realize their paths could break in opposite directions at any time now.

"This changes things for me," Dalton said quietly.

He had no idea if she'd heard him, was speechless or just plain old didn't feel the same way.

THE SHERIFF'S REFUSAL to meet with Leanne gave her no choice but to show up at his office. Thankfully, the baby was safe at the ranch. Mila's presence seemed to distract Hampton and Bethany, too. Her sister had lit up when she saw Mila, constantly expressing how much she'd wanted to visit after the birth.

It seemed that Bethany was channeling some of her extra energy into Mila. Her sister was brighter today and Leanne hoped it was because she wasn't taking the medication that blanked her face and the fact that she'd made a decision not to go back to Gary.

"I need to speak to the sheriff. It's urgent," Leanne said as Janis, the sheriff's receptionist, came around her desk with her hands out in front of her.

"Hold on there. Slow down a minute." The older woman had a kind but firm way about her. She was tall, close to six feet if Leanne had to guess. And she was using every inch of her height to block the hallway leading to Sawmill's office.

"Let him know I'm here, and I'm sure he'll agree to see me," she defended.

Dalton was behind her, but he didn't seem to have a play.

Since making love, his normally tense expression had relaxed and he was even more attractive. She'd let his last words sit between them, unsure of what they meant or what either of them could do about them, anyway. Her life was in Dallas and his in Cattle Barge.

Leanne had a daughter who would always be her priority. Trying to add someone else to the equation of her already-complicated life seemed like looking for disaster. She couldn't make the math work, no matter how much her heart wanted to argue.

Cattle Barge was hours away from Dallas. Dalton loved the land he lived on. Their lifestyles were on the opposite end of the spectrum. She had a job that required long hours and a child who deserved her attention when she wasn't working. As much as Leanne loved her mother, there were many times she felt left out when her mother was seeing someone new. Eating dinners alone before the age of twelve was about the saddest thing she remembered.

Leanne needed Mila to know she came first.

A little voice in her head said circumstances were completely different. Mila was a baby. But then that made things even worse. What was she supposed to say to Dalton? "Hold on while I burp my baby"? "Sorry, she just threw up on your good pants"? None of it worked.

And yet, when his hand came up to her shoulder, everything scrambled in her logical mind and she wished they could give a relationship a shot.

Didn't he say that working a ranch was a seven-day-week job?

"Please let me in there," she begged.

Janis studied her for a long moment. "I can't do that or I might lose my job."

Leanne started to argue, but Janis's hand came up again. "You seem like the kind of person who won't take *no* for an answer." She craned her neck like she was using her head to point to the back parking lot. "And he's due any minute. He'll most likely come through that back door." More of the head movements. "And there's not much I can do if someone wants to wait out there on public property in order to speak to him."

It dawned on Leanne that Janis was actually helping her out.

"My job wouldn't be hurt at all. Nothing in my file—"

She didn't need to finish her sentence, because she was already shushing them out the front door. Leanne understood.

"Thank you," she mouthed, careful not to say it too loud.

"No one's ever thanked me for kicking them out before," she said a little too loudly, and Leanne knew it was for the benefit of anyone who was trying to listen to their conversation.

Bolting around the station, Leanne caught the sheriff as he opened the back door.

Chapter Fifteen

"Sheriff Sawmill," she shouted to get his attention as she rounded the corner, desperate to get to him before he pretended not to see her and slipped inside the door.

"I'm on a case right now, Detective West." His tone was irritated, but he rested his hand on the half-opened door.

"We'd like to speak to you about the victims—"

"We've already been over this," he insisted. "I sent a report to your supervisor this afternoon."

"I haven't spoken to my SO today," she admitted. "Dal—Mr. Butler and I have been thinking and we'd like you to hear us out."

Sawmill glanced around as a reporter dashed around the corner. Normally, she didn't appreciate media interfering but in this case, it might actually help her out.

"Come inside," he said after a second.

"Thank you, sir." Leanne knew she was putting her job on the line.

Sawmill led them inside his office and closed the door behind them. "I'm willing to hear you out this time but make no mistake about it, this is a favor."

"Understood," Leanne said, grateful to have the sheriff's ear.

He didn't sit down, so neither did they. She pulled out a notepad from her purse.

"Dalton and I have been looking at the cases from a different angle, trying to infuse another approach," she started.

"I've already—"

"Come on, sheriff," Dalton interrupted. "You can't tell me these cases don't look enough alike to at least make you question it."

Sawmill nodded in response. "I'm already thinking the same thing."

"Hear what she has to say. If you don't agree, the only thing you've lost is a couple minutes of your time," Dalton continued.

"Okay. I'm listening."

"The bodies showed no signs of putting up a fight. So, it's possible they were drugged and that's why there are no signs of struggle. The victims are both a little more than five-feet-tall blondes, both seventeen years old. They were hung from the same tree on the same night fourteen years apart," she said.

"Tell me something I don't know," Sawmill responded with an even tone.

"I made a few phone calls last night and found out that one of the bus drivers at the high school has a biology degree," Dalton said. "He quit his job and moved home after his mother died."

"Ted Brown has a biology degree?" Sawmill asked.

"He's strong enough to carry the victims," Dalton said. "He was twenty-six when the first victim was hanged. Forty years old now and strong as an ox."

"One of my deputies collected coke caps from the underbrush at the scene. Maybe we'll get a DNA hit," the sheriff said.

"Ted doesn't have a record that I know of," Dalton said. "I didn't know him personally, but people said he came back from school after an accident. Said he hasn't quite been right ever since."

"I checked the database and didn't get any hits for other victims on December 7," Sawmill admitted.

"It's not uncommon for a serial killer to have a cooling-off period," Leanne chimed in. "He would need to have other victims, of course, to fit this classification."

"Seems like someone with a mental impairment or brain injury would have a difficult time pulling off two murders without leaving a trail," Sawmill said. It was true that most killers had low IQs and were caught early as a result. It was also true that the really smart ones literally got away with murder.

"I believe he's showing off. He thinks he's superior, so he's rubbing our noses in it," Leanne stated. "The trucker's knot. The public display. He wanted the victims to be found, because he's thumbing his nose at us."

"You don't believe your brother-in-law is involved?" Sawmill asked.

"If he is, throw the damn book at him. I just can't reconcile it. He's a hothead, my brother-in-law. I found out he's been physically rough with my sister a few times." She flashed her eyes at the sheriff. "Believe me, I had no idea any of this was going on. They kept me in the dark. I'm guessing they knew what my reaction would be."

"Which would be understandable, but that doesn't solve my case."

"Yes. But right now I'm thinking my brother-in-law is your best suspect and you can see the holes in that theory better than I can. You have another higher-profile murder investigation sitting on your back and while you figure out who did that, you need this win as badly as we do." Leanne didn't hold back, and she hoped it wouldn't get them kicked out.

The sheriff took a step closer and looked at the notepad she was holding.

"You believe the suspect is male. Strong. Brown is at the top of your list," he said. "But Bartholomew, the druggist's son, is on there, too. The man has a family. Goes to church on Sunday."

"So did the BTK Killer. Having a family and going to church didn't stop him from stalking and killing women," Leanne interjected.

"But you want access to Brown."

"Yes. But I can't touch him without putting the case in jeopardy, and I won't do anything that might damage your investigation." She studied Sawmill. Tired? Check. Listening? Check.

This was the most progress she'd made with him since they met a few days ago. Had it really only been a handful of days? Barely sleeping for most of it stretched the days into what felt like weeks. It was impossible that she and Dalton had only known each other for a short time. Her feelings for him ran deeper than anything she'd known before. A little voice reminded her that they were in an intense situation and that could bring out all kinds of extra hormones.

Was it hormones? Really?

A blind attraction that would fade?

She hoped not, because she'd felt struck by a stray lightning bolt from the minute she met the handsome cowboy. Getting to know him only made her respect him even more. He was the kind of guy she could see herself with long term under different circumstances. If the relationship had time to take hold before she returned to the city.

Long distance rarely worked without all the complications they had. Leanne didn't have it in her heart to try again with anyone.

Did she?

"THIS IS GOOD investigative work," Sawmill finally said after they gave him a few more choices for suspects. He folded his arms.

Dalton knew that he was also signaling that it was time to end the meeting.

"We appreciate your time, Sheriff," he said, offering a handshake.

This meeting was going a long way toward rebuilding trust and the sheriff seemed to realize it when he took the outstretched hand in a firm grasp.

"Can I take a picture of that page?" Sawmill asked.

"Absolutely," Leanne said with pride.

Dalton liked it when she smiled. He wanted to talk to her about the possibility of spending time together once she returned to Dallas. He'd shelve the thought for now, but his chest was lighter than it had been in longer than he could remember. The chinks in his armor, allowing some of the pain to seep out, had the benefit of him carrying a lighter load.

"I'll follow up on these leads and see where these people were on the seventh," Sawmill promised.

The pair stood after thanking the sheriff.

Dalton walked Leanne to the SUV, stopping to give her a kiss before opening her door.

"You think she's still asleep?" Leanne asked, referring to her daughter. "I want to call and check on her, but I don't want to wake anyone."

"Let's give it a minute," he said. "Besides, I have an idea."

The smile on Leanne's face broke down more of the casing around his heart. He was falling. Hard. He just hoped there'd be a life raft when she walked away.

He didn't tell her where they were going, but it wasn't far out of town. The two chatted easily on the way. Leanne seemed pleased the sheriff was taking them seriously and he couldn't deny that he was, too.

It was Christmastime and his turn to bring

home the tree. The Butlers had a tradition that no other decorations could go up inside without first having a tree.

Dalton realized something about the sheriff through this process. Sawmill had a tough job. He had a lot of pride in his work and even if he made a mistake, it wasn't because he didn't care. There was an odd comfort in the sentiment.

"Okay," he finally said. "We're almost there."

"Great, because all I see is farm road," she quipped. There was a lightness to her voice that he liked. Was it because they were making progress in the case? He figured that was part of it. Seeing her daughter had improved her mood considerably. And then they'd made love.

Dalton couldn't remember when it had been so right. He wanted to make Leanne happy.

"You were talking about feeling like a failure earlier for not being more prepared for your daughter's first Christmas," he began as he winded down the path.

"Yes. So, why are we out in the sticks? I thought the ranch was remote until you brought me out here. Is there even cell reception?" She checked her phone for bars.

"Maybe. Maybe not," he teased.

"Tell me again why we're all the way out here," she pleaded.

"Hold on," he said. And then he rounded the

bend, revealing the best Christmas tree farm in Texas. "Here."

"This…is…beautiful." She wiped a tear.

"There's no need to get emotional," he said, but his chest swelled with pride.

"I've never been to a real Christmas tree farm before. When Mila is older, I want to bring her back here."

There were more pines than he could count. He parked the SUV and hopped out so he could open her door for her.

"This is…" She seemed to be searching for the right word. She also seemed at a loss, so he kissed her.

She responded in a way that got him aroused. Bad idea out here. And when he looked up afterward, he smiled when he saw mistletoe hanging over the trellis leading to trail to the small forest.

"You ready to pick out your first Christmas tree for your daughter?" he asked. Leanne deserved this. So did Mila. The kid was as cute as a button. He briefly envisioned bringing them here for hayrides and hot chocolate as Mila grew older.

"Can we get any one of these?" Leanne took off running toward the plantings. This close to Christmas the lot had a fair amount of vehicles, mostly trucks.

Dalton hoped he had a way to tie off whatever tree she picked as he chased her through the forest of evergreens.

"What do we do?" she finally asked, out of breath, as she stopped in front of one.

"Get an ax," he said.

"No." She spun around, grabbed him and pulled him closer until he could breathe the same air as her. "They're too perfect. I don't want to spoil them by taking an ax to one."

"I can understand your point," he said, tugging her toward him. "I can."

He could feel her heartbeat against his chest. Hers pounded from the run, and it reminded him of another time her pulse raced alongside his.

"But this family grows these trees as a source of income. This land is dedicated to growing trees to be chopped down, so it's not hurting the environment. In fact, it's helping out a very good family," he explained before kissing her again. The taste of convenience-store coffee was still on her breath from when they'd stopped earlier to pick up a couple of cups.

"Need any help?" A bear of a man walked toward them. He couldn't be much more than forty years old.

"Dalton Butler." He stuck out his hand.

"Hardy." The man gripped his hand and Dalton was immediately aware of the strength in his handshake.

"Do you work for the Santanas?" Dalton asked. He didn't remember seeing Hardy around before.

"Pamela's my aunt," he said by way of explanation. He wore lumberjack-type clothing and wielded a hefty-sized ax. He wore a serious expression and something darkened his eyes as his gaze landed on the area of Leanne's shoulder holster. "You like this one here?"

"Yes." Dalton pulled Leanne closer to him. It was probably just because the guy almost matched him in height and build, and was wielding an ax that caused him to want to keep her within arm's reach. Primal instinct. Nothing more. "You live here, too?"

"Nah. Just come when I can get away from home. My uncle's getting up there in years and Pamela can use a hand." Hardy shrugged, pulled the ax sideways and then got off his first shot at the trunk. He had the form of a professional golfer with similar precision. Wood chips flew from the contact as he made a large dent in the side of the tree. He turned to Dalton and Leanne. "You might want to step back."

He tagged the tree before pulling a slip of paper out of his pocket and handing it to Leanne. Something else flashed behind his eyes, but it happened so fast Dalton couldn't be sure.

Dalton put his body in between Hardy and Leanne, linking their fingers as they took a few steps back.

A few hacks at the trunk later and Hardy hauled the tree up onto his shoulder. "What are you driving?"

"Sport utility. Black." Dalton supplied the license plate number.

"Take that slip I gave you to my aunt to pay. I'll have this strapped to your vehicle by the time she runs the charge," Hardy said.

"Will do," Dalton replied.

"I've never had a real Christmas tree before," Leanne admitted when they were out of earshot.

"There's nothing like waking up to the smell of pine to tell you the holiday is here." Dalton had mixed feelings about this year and that was most likely the reason he'd been stalling on finding a tree. Then again, it was his turn this year and he'd been dreading it. Being with Leanne, seeing her eyes light up when she saw "the one" gave him a warm feeling in his chest. Was that cold heart of his finally thawing out? It had been frozen for a very long time. *Too long*, a little voice in his head said. The voice sounded a whole helluva lot like Alexandria's.

Deep down, he knew she'd want him to be happy. In the past, attempts to reclaim his life had felt hollow. Not this time. Not with Leanne.

She squeezed his hand with the excitement of a little kid. But the kiss she planted on his lips next was all woman. It also got something stirring they couldn't deal with out here in the cold.

He smiled at her and she seemed to catch on. The sparkle in her eyes told him all he needed to know about what she was thinking, too.

"Thank you," she said, looking right through him to his core. "I haven't felt this happy, this alive in longer than I can remember."

"Me, either." Happiness had always been fleeting in Dalton's life. And he feared this time would be no different. Yes, his feelings ran deep for the woman at his side, as they linked their fingers again and strolled through the pine forest. But they'd be out of the woods and back to reality soon.

The small wood hut at the entrance to the gravel parking lot had a window for transactions.

"Pamela," Dalton said as he walked up. She was short. He couldn't see much more than her platinum blond hair, which was piled on top of her head when he first approached.

"In the flesh," she chirped.

She wore too much blue eye shadow over brown eyes and had a nice but worn dimpled smile.

"Hardy said I should give you this." He handed over the slip of paper.

"Excellent choice," she said, looking over the small sheet. "A nine-foot Leyland cypress. That's my favorite kind." She looked harder at him. "I'm sorry I can't keep you and your brother straight. Are you Dalton?"

"Guilty," he admitted, pulling out his money clip and peeling off a few twenties after hearing the price.

"It's a pleasure to see you again. I'm real sorry about your papa," she said, taking the bills being offered. Her eyes widened. "This is too much."

"Give whatever's left over to Hardy."

"He'll appreciate it," she said on a sigh. "As a boy, he went through more than anyone should have to endure in one lifetime. For a while, I thought he wouldn't come out the other side after witnessing his mother bring man after man parading through the home, each one with his own set of problems. There were severe punishments that…let's just say that each new male figure seemed to have a new way to torture Hardy. Later on, he got into trouble but he learned his lesson while he served his time," she glanced up and seemed to have revealed more than she'd wanted to, "and here he is."

"I'm sorry to hear about his past. Nice of him to help out," Dalton said, noticing she'd called Hardy a boy instead of a man.

"It gives him running money." Pamela flashed eyes at him. "Sorry, I shouldn't talk about other people's problems."

"I thought I knew everyone in Cattle Barge," Dalton added. "Did he grow up around here?"

"No. He's not from around these parts. Me and my husband bought this farm fourteen years ago to make a fresh start after he lost his job." Pamela had a wistful look on her face, but she reined it in real quick and then handed him a receipt. "You folks have a nice holiday. Come back and see us next year."

"We will. And you, too." Dalton took the paper and stuffed it inside his front pocket.

He and Leanne walked to his sport utility as another car pulled into the parking lot. Hardy was already tying another tree on top of a sedan. The place seemed to do a steady business.

On the road again, something was bugging Dalton.

Chapter Sixteen

"I have a weird feeling." Leanne hadn't been able to shake it since she and Dalton left the tree farm.

"Same here."

They'd winded down the lane and onto the road leading toward the highway.

"Can't put my finger on it," she admitted. "Did Hardy rub you the wrong way?"

"He did."

A few seconds later, Dalton mashed the brake and pulled onto the shoulder of the two-lane road. He bolted out of the SUV and released a string of swear words.

"What is it?" she asked.

"Check the sign," he said.

She glanced around the road and locked on to a sign. They were on Farm Road 1207. Immediately, 12-07 shot to mind. The date.

Leanne flew out of the vehicle, because she

knew exactly what he was doing. Checking the knot.

"Is it the same one?" she asked.

"Yes," Dalton said after muttering a few more curse words. The same ones she was thinking. He pulled a slip out of his pocket and then muttered more. "His aunt mentioned that he'd served time. Could explain why there haven't been any murders in between Alexandria and Clara."

"She also mentioned something about a traumatic childhood and not being from around here," she said.

"And that he had a whole mess to deal with back at home."

"There's always a trigger with serial killers," Leanne added as anger filled her.

"Get in." Dalton was already reclaiming his seat.

"No, Dalton. Stop. Whatever you're thinking is the wrong move." She knew based on his actions that he wanted to go back and spend a few minutes alone with Hardy. "We don't have proof and as much as I want to hurt him, if he's the one responsible, we'll only do more damage if we go vigilante."

Dalton was the kind of man who was used to taking care of business himself. It was one of the attributes she admired most about him.

"I'm going back to ask a few more questions." His white-knuckle grip on the steering wheel intensified.

"Let's think this through first." Sure, his anger was running high now. And she wanted revenge as much as he must. "We want the same things."

"Then get in and put on your seat belt." His voice was a low rumble.

"If he's guilty, I want him to pay for the rest of his life, Dalton. I want him thrown behind bars so he can remember every day what he's done. We go back there, find out it's him and take his life, then what? He's gone. It's over for him. I want him to suffer for the rest of his life."

Dalton stared out the windshield, but she could see that her words were making an impact.

"Let's do this instead. Let's call the sheriff and tell him what's going on," she said.

"What if it's him? What if he runs and they don't catch him? He'll continue to walk free. He'll hurt more girls and a helluva lot sooner this time." The anger was still very much present in his words, but she was chipping away at his emotions by using logic. Dalton was a logical man. If she could continue to appeal to that side of him, she had a chance at doing this the right way.

"They'll go after him. They'll find him. And if they don't, we will."

"But I'm right here. I can take care of this right now. I can make sure that bastard never sees another sunset. As long as he's breathing and free, he'll find another target." The intensity of his voice softened ever so slightly, but she could tell she was making headway.

"Let's make the call. Do this the right way. He isn't going anywhere. He doesn't suspect a thing, Dalton. We have the element of surprise on our side, and Christmas isn't for a few weeks. He'll be right here. And now that the sheriff will know what he's looking for, he'll build a solid case that will make sure he doesn't see daylight for the rest of his life."

Dalton sat there, grinding his back teeth. She knew that the man in him wanted to take Hardy in his bare hands and squeeze the life out of him for what he'd done. It was primal, but Dalton was a good man. She had to believe that he'd act on reason. Or maybe if she was honest with him, she could give him a better emotional reason.

"I have a selfish reason for not wanting you to circle back, Dalton. I'm falling for you, hard. I've never felt this way about another man, and I want to figure out a way to see each other when this is all over. I can admit that I don't know how it'll work with our lives, but I want to try. See where this thing goes. I want us to have a chance. And we can't do that if you're behind bars."

His gaze intensified on the road ahead. Finally, he ground out, "Make the call. Ask Sawmill if anyone saw pine needles around the parking lot or the tree."

Leanne wouldn't look a gift horse in the mouth, and her heart leapt at the thought that he might want the same things.

He'd already pulled his cell out and he was checking the photos from the scene.

She wasted no time retrieving her cell from her purse and making the call to Sawmill. She intentionally left her door open so that Dalton couldn't change his mind without talking to her first.

"They're right there." He cursed and showed her a picture of the base of the tree with pine needles nearby.

After relaying this new information to the sheriff, she ended the call and looked at Dalton. "He's putting every available resource toward tracking down what happened to Hardy and his family. And Sawmill is on his way."

"I need to go back and look him in the eyes right now," Dalton said, his intensity returned. "I can't walk away when I'm this close, Leanne."

DALTON STALKED TOWARD the trees. If he cut a path straight through them, he could get to Hardy within minutes. Anger fueled his steps; fourteen years it had built up inside him like a simmering volcano, and he'd finally found the release valve.

Hardy needed to pay for what he'd done.

"Dalton, stop," Leanne called after him, and he could tell she wasn't far behind. Her voice broke through the ringing noise in his ears.

So much anger. So much pain. And the reason stood a football field away.

"We don't have all the facts yet." Leanne's voice sounded desperate. And that dented some of his armor.

"I know all I need to." He stomped through the underbrush of the nongroomed area of the tree farm.

"Please, stop," she continued. "If we do this the wrong way, he could go scot-free. I know you don't want that any more than I do. If you assault Hardy, you'll be the one in trouble. The sheriff will be here any minute. Alexandria wouldn't want you to go to jail, Dalton."

Those words slowed his pace.

"From what I can gather, the two of you cared a great deal about each other. Ask yourself if this is what she would wish for you." Damn those words were having an effect on him.

Maybe it would be better to think this through instead of acting on his rage. Thinking back, no good had ever come out of his making a decision or reacting from anger.

At this point, he didn't care what happened to him—although that wasn't completely true now that he'd found Leanne—but she made good points about Alexandria. One of the things he'd loved so much about her was her compassion.

The feeling of an explosion rocketed his chest.

Leanne was right. Alexandria wouldn't want this.

Hardy deserved to spend the rest of his life in jail. He deserved to face punishment for what he'd done. He deserved to suffer for the innocent lives he'd cut short. He deserved to wake up every day knowing the pain he'd caused.

Taking in a sharp breath, he spun around. His action wasn't fast enough to react to the large sharp rock being hurled at his head.

And then he blacked out.

DALTON BLINKED HIS eyes open. He lay sprawled out on the ground. His head hurt and his eyes burned. He brought his hand up to his forehead and immediately drew it back. Pain shot through him as everything came back to him in a jolt. *Leanne.*

Footsteps sounded nearby. More than one pair? Running away or coming toward him?

He'd been too caught up in his own anger before to realize they were being hunted. He forced himself upright and scanned the area. *She* was being hunted. Clearly, Leanne was the one Hardy wanted, considering she was nowhere in sight.

The sounds of footsteps drew closer. Was Hardy coming back for round two in order to finish him off?

Dizziness made it difficult to get to his feet. A burst of adrenaline helped but nausea quickly followed. He stabilized himself by grabbing hold of a tree trunk.

A man in a brown uniform moved through the trees. Dalton recognized the sheriff immediately.

"Over here," he said loud enough to get the sheriff's attention and hopefully no one else's. It occurred to Dalton a few moments too late that Hardy would know this land better than anyone else.

Sawmill shifted his direction toward the sound of Dalton's voice. His eyes widened when he got close enough to look at him.

"I'll call for an ambulance," he said.

Dalton had ignored the liquid he felt running down the side of his face. He touched it and drew back his hand, his fingers now covered in blood.

"I'm fine," he said. "He got Leanne."

Deputy Granger came up behind the sheriff. He'd stood back and had been surveying the area.

"It's clear," he said.

"The address to the tree farm is 14 Pine Lane. The farm road is 1207. He hung both girls in a tree. And now the bastard has Leanne," Dalton said.

"Let's secure the area and interview the aunt and uncle," Sawmill said.

"She said something traumatic happened in his past and that he's served time." Hardy could've taken Leanne anywhere on the property. He could've killed her already and buried her.

"Moved from where?" Sawmill asked.

"She didn't say."

"I want that interview now," Sawmill barked.

Pamela was still in the shack with a small line of customers when they arrived a few minutes later.

"What happened?" she immediately asked, her gaze flying to Dalton's forehead and the fresh blood. She burst out the side door. "Follow me. I have a first aid kit in the house."

She must've thought Dalton had brought the

sheriff back to have her arrested based on how scared she looked.

"We're looking for your nephew, Hardy," Sawmill said.

She stopped in her tracks.

"What did he do?" Her question was peculiar. There didn't seem to be any doubt in her mind that he deserved to be arrested. More warning flares lit in Dalton's mind.

"You said he served time. What was his crime?" Dalton asked.

"Drugs." Her gaze bounced from the sheriff to Dalton.

She stared toward the sky. "I thought he cleaned up his act. He found religion and—"

"When was he released?" A picture was emerging that clenched Dalton's stomach.

"Six months ago."

"Is he here?" Sawmill was surveying the area.

"I haven't seen him, and that's why I have a line of customers waiting to be helped." She motioned toward the shack. "I need to fetch my husband."

"Ma'am, we need your cooperation. We believe that your nephew has taken a female law enforcement officer hostage." Sawmill's voice had a sense of urgency.

"Norman," she called out.

"Ma'am, do you know where he is?" Sawmill continued, trying to direct her back onto the right path.

"No, I don't. I wish I did. This is bad." She shook her head and tears welled. "We knew something was wrong, but we thought he was holding it together. You say he took a woman?"

"Yes."

"He hates law enforcement after what happened," she confessed. "He's always talking about making them pay. About them being too stupid." She flashed her eyes at Sawmill and Deputy Granger. "I'm sorry. They were his words, not mine."

"What happened?"

"His younger sister was abducted when she was seventeen by their mother's boyfriend. She was found before he killed her..." Pamela made apologetic eyes at them for needing a minute. "But she couldn't adapt after the ordeal and a few weeks later, on December 7, she hung herself. Hardy found her," she said. "He blamed the way law enforcement handled her case for her suicide. He never did get over it. He got so sad. I guess he used drugs to numb his pain. We had no idea he'd do anything like this or we never would've brought him here."

Sawmill steadied himself, because it looked like his legs were about to give. "He killed two girls, both seventeen years old, and fourteen years apart."

Sawmill cursed, and it was the first time Dalton saw the man almost lose his composure. He regained his footing and jumped into action.

Within the hour, law enforcement had descended on the surrounding area, searching for Leanne by air, four-wheelers and on foot. Calling her phone was the first thing they'd tried. She couldn't be tracked using GPS, either. Hardy must've disarmed her. If she had control of her weapon or her cell phone Dalton would've heard from her by now.

There was no sign of her or Hardy.

"I put out a 'be on the lookout,' a BOLO. I'll put in a call to Texas State Troopers in order to warn them personally in case he's on the highway somewhere."

"I need to talk to her sister and tell her what's going on." Dalton knew Bethany would be worried. She knew Leanne wouldn't disappear without checking in with her since Mila was there. "Call me if you get a hit?"

It would be breaking protocol, but it was worth a shot to ask the sheriff.

"I'll let you know the second we get anything," Sawmill promised.

Dalton hitched a ride back to his SUV, which

was parked on the side of the road. He thanked the deputy before taking off.

The road in front of him seemed to stretch on for mile after empty mile. Darkness covered the land. At this time of evening, there weren't many vehicles on the highway.

And then a thought struck.

This was personal. While all available resources were at the tree farm, Hardy had the perfect opportunity to deliver a devastating blow to Sawmill.

Dalton bit down a curse and jammed his foot onto the gas pedal.

Chapter Seventeen

Dalton had a hunch that Hardy would take Leanne to the tree. He just didn't know if she'd be dead or alive.

Instead of banking a left on the farm road that would take him to Hereford, he turned the wheel right. He made good time back to Cattle Barge.

Driving up to the spot when it was still dark outside would make his headlights give him away. It seemed like the surest way to get Leanne killed.

His stomach lining braided thinking about what could have happened to her already. He knew he shouldn't go there.

Whatever was going on, he'd face it.

For three hours he camped out near the tree.

Dalton found a place to watch. Seeing the tree was difficult but he'd see anyone walking up to it. The sheriff and his deputies were canvassing neighboring ranches around the tree farm and checking out the list of possible hiding places that Pamela had supplied.

A burst of adrenaline shot through Dalton as he inched closer and saw Leanne's limp body hanging from the oak tree. Dalton palmed his weapon. Hardy was there. From this distance, he could see that Hardy was supporting her weight, using his shoulder as he tied the knot around her neck.

Dread was a hard knock as Dalton faced the very real fear that she might already be dead.

But then he remembered what she'd said about ketamine and a burst of hope filled his chest that she was out and not gone.

Hardy most likely had her gun but his hands were currently full, which played to Dalton's advantage.

Biting back a curse, Dalton bolted out of the woods. He covered the distance between them in a few quick strides before diving toward Hardy's knees.

Making contact, Dalton drove Hardy a step back and heard a loud crack. A bone?

Fighting back, Dalton connected a fist with Hardy's jaw. Another crack.

And that's where Dalton's advantage ended.

With an animal-like grunt, Hardy pounded his fists against Dalton's body, connecting with his ribs, arms and face.

Leanne hung in the tree a few feet away behind him, and Dalton feared no matter how quickly he subdued Hardy, it would be too late for her.

Fourteen years of rage exploded inside him and, just like a bomb detonating, he exploded against his enemy. On the man who had taken so much from him.

Dalton pounded his fists against Hardy, delivering punch after punch in rapid succession. He worked on Hardy's gut and face until the man threw his arms up to block. Putting Hardy on the defensive, gaining ground, Dalton pummeled harder.

Thoughts of Alexandria—her pure smile, her sweet personality—tore through him like an out-of-control storm. And then, there were his feelings for Leanne--feelings that ran steady and deep.

Hardy wrestled Dalton for control, managed to get it. Anger surged and Dalton flipped the big guy on his back again. The guy was pinned, momentarily secure, but Dalton was paralyzed. One wrong move and Hardy would gain the upper hand. And if he didn't get to Leanne soon, it would be too late.

The image of her limp body dangling from that tree momentarily distracted him. Hardy landed a punch that most likely broke Dalton's nose and threw him off balance enough to tip the scale in Hardy's favor.

Hardy bucked, knocking Dalton off him.

And then Hardy launched into a terror of flying fists, grabbing and punching anywhere and everywhere on Dalton's bruised body.

Dalton captured Hardy's right hand and rolled several times, separating himself for a brief moment.

Hardy flew toward Dalton and as he was about to land on top of him, Dalton threw a punch, his fist connected with the man's face, jutting it awkwardly to the left.

When Hardy landed, he lay in a lump on the ground. Dalton's gaze flew toward the tree as he forced himself upright. His twin brother, Dade, was running toward Leanne.

"She's alive," Dade said. "She freed herself before I got here."

Leanne had propped herself up, and she was leaning against the trunk.

Dalton looked at the tree that had taken so much from him.

But not this time.

"An ambulance is on the way," Dade said as he made it to Dalton's side and offered a hand up. "Let's get you over to her."

"She's alive," Dalton repeated softly as a surprising tear leaked from his eye.

"You did it," Dade reassured as he helped Dalton to Leanne. "I stopped by to bring food before starting my workday and saw it unfold. You did it, Dalton."

Dalton was too exhausted to say much. He took Leanne's hand as Dade said he'd keep watch over Hardy's body until authorities arrived.

Leanne's face was pale and her breathing shallow.

"Please don't leave me, Leanne," he whispered, adding, "I know how crazy this might sound but I love you."

LEANNE WOKE IN unfamiliar surroundings. She blinked her eyes open with a gasp as memories of being abducted by Hardy came back in a flash. She pushed up to a sitting position and looked around the room, steadying her rapid heartbeat.

The sun was blazing in the sky. She threw her feet over the side of the bed, checked to make sure she had clothes on. Exhaled a slow breath when she saw that she did.

She had to remind herself that she wasn't in the freezing cave that Hardy had dragged her into and kept her in a drug-induced haze for days. She'd spent several more in the hospital before being released.

And then remembered where she was. The Hereford Ranch. But this wasn't the bedroom she'd slept in.

She managed to get to her feet on shaky legs. A bathrobe was on a chair next to the bed. She slipped the white cotton robe on and tied the belt. A toothbrush waited for her in an adjacent bathroom and she was so grateful. It tasted like she'd slept with cotton balls in her mouth. She was so thirsty she bent down to take a drink from the faucet and then splashed some cold water on her face.

Commotion in the bedroom caused her to turn a little too fast. She gripped the doorjamb to steady herself and was glad she did when she saw Dalton holding Mila. Her daughter was cooing at him and she'd never seen him look so happy.

The expression morphed when he saw her standing there. "You should be in bed."

"How long was I asleep?" she asked.

"Not long enough. The doctor said it'll take a few more days before you start feeling like yourself again," he informed.

Her concern melted a little when she looked at her happy baby. Mila was all smiles.

"We did it, Dalton," Leanne said, remembering that Hardy would go to jail for the rest of his life with the evidence against him.

"We sure did."

She leaned into him and cried.

When there were no tears left, he helped her onto the edge of the bed.

"I can't bring her back," she said on a sob.

"I know."

Mila made a cooing noise at her mother and Leanne smiled through her tears.

"You want a cup of coffee?" Dalton had several days' worth of scruff on his chin, but his face was more relaxed than she'd ever seen.

"Sounds like heaven, actually," she said, wanting to hold her baby but afraid she wasn't strong enough yet. "Have you slept much?"

"Me?" he scoffed, and it made her laugh. "I don't sleep. I've been setting up a scholarship for Christian. I hope you don't mind, but I set it up in honor of Clara and it bears her name."

"She would've loved that," Leanne admitted. She looked at her baby. "I wish I could hold her."

"You could sit on the floor," he said.

Leanne leaned on his free arm for support, anchoring herself against his strong biceps and the bed as she sat down. She stretched out sore legs.

He set Mila next to her with a pillow behind the little girl's back for support.

"I'll be right back." He feathered a kiss on Leanne's forehead before jetting out of the room.

Dalton returned, as promised, a few minutes later with two mugs of coffee and joined them on the floor.

Leanne immediately took a sip. It tasted perfect. Being here with Dalton and Mila was perfect. But perfect had a shelf life.

"This might sound crazy, but hear me out." Dalton flashed his eyes at her. "In the past few days, I've fallen for you, Leanne. I'm all in. Your daughter is the most beautiful baby, but don't tell my brother that." He smiled and it warmed her heart. Was he saying what she was hoping? That they'd somehow figure out a way to see each other after going back to their lives. A life that felt hollow somehow without Dalton in it.

"We might've just met, but I feel like I've known you my entire life. I see how hard you fight for what you believe in, for the people you love. And that's all it takes to make a relationship work. I want you to know that if you have the same feelings for me, if you love me, I have every intention of asking you to marry me."

Warmth cascaded over Leanne at the sound of those words.

"I do love you, Dalton. I can't imagine living

one more day without you in my life," she said. "So, what are you waiting for?"

A slow smile spread across his lips.

"I promise to love this little girl and protect her as the child of my heart that she is. And I vow to live each day to bring a smile to your lips and make sure you know how much I cherish you. Leanne West, will you do me the honor of being my wife and making the three of us a family?"

"Yes." Tears of happiness and joy spilled down her face. "I will marry you, Dalton."

Dalton leaned over and kissed her. Mila giggled at the wonder of her own hand and the two of them laughed with her.

After playing on the floor without having to watch the clock, hunger finally made its presence known. "I could eat for two days straight right now."

"Wanting food is a good sign," he said with a smile.

"How's my sister?" she asked, needing to know what she'd be facing when she walked down that hallway.

"She's good. She's been hanging around with May and spending time with Hampton. He's loving it here, and there's talk in the family of finding a permanent job for Bethany and setting her up with a place to stay."

"Has she mentioned Gary?" She hiked a brow.

"Yes," he admitted. "You should know that Gary admitted to hiring a guy to go to the park in Dallas, but he swears he never had any intention of actually taking the baby. He was trying to scare you and get you to go home so he could work on Bethany. He knows it was stupid. He turned himself in to the sheriff."

Leanne took a minute to let that sink in. Gary wasn't the brightest and she could see him following down that path of logic, crazy as it was. "Is he being held?"

"Our family lawyer put a call in to the judge who said they wanted to sweat him out. Give him a couple of days to really think about what he's done," Dalton said.

"Serves him right. But it would be best for my sister and Hampton if Gary got his act together," Leanne admitted after careful thought. "I'm not saying I think she should go back to him after he got physical with her. But he needs to learn to be a better man."

"Ella is certain she can reform anyone if she has the right resources and they're willing. He says he is, but Bethany said he's going to have to change big-time and prove he's worth another shot before he's allowed to be in the same room with her or their son again. It'll take time for her to trust him. Losing his family and Clara seems to have finally sunk in."

"Whether he's in the picture at some point or not, at least my sister's on the right track," she said.

"We all know what it's like to grow up without a father. No one's giving up on helping Gary become the man he needs to be. Whether they all live in the same house or not will be up to them when the time is right. For now, he's willing to work on himself and earn the right to be a father and husband again."

Warmth spread through her at hearing those words.

People deserved second chances.

Dalton made a move to get up, but she touched his arm. "Did you get the answers you were looking for about your relationship with your father?"

"Don't need 'em." There was so much sincerity in his eyes when he looked at her. "I already have the two of you."

With that, she tilted her head toward the sky and kissed her future husband, the man she loved with her whole heart, the man who was her home.

* * * * *

Look for the next book in
USA Today *Bestselling Author Barb Han's*
Crisis: Cattle Barge miniseries,
Bulletproof Christmas,
available next month.

And don't miss the previous titles
in the Crisis: Cattle Barge series:

Sudden Setup
Endangered Heiress
Texas Grit
Kidnapped at Christmas

Available now from Harlequin Intrigue!

Get 4 FREE REWARDS!

We'll send you 2 FREE Books plus 2 FREE Mystery Gifts.

Harlequin Presents® books feature a sensational and sophisticated world of international romance where sinfully tempting heroes ignite passion.

FREE Value Over **$20**

READERSERVICE.COM

Manage your account online!

- Review your order history
- Manage your payments
- Update your address

> *We've designed the*
> *Reader Service website*
> *just for you.*

Enjoy all the features!

- Discover new series available to you, and read excerpts from any series.
- Respond to mailings and special monthly offers.
- Browse the Bonus Bucks catalog and online-only exculsives.
- Share your feedback.

Visit us at:

ReaderService.com